I0578703

TO ANY LENGTHS

Books by Jacqueline Gay Walley

'Venus As She Ages' Collection of Novels:

Strings Attached (Second Edition, Gay Walley)

To Any Lengths

Prison Sex

The Bed You Lie In

Write, She Said

Magnetism

Books by Gay Walley

Novels:

Strings Attached (First Edition)

The Erotic Fire of the Unattainable

Lost in Montreal

Duet

E-Books on Bookboon:

The Smart Guide to Business Writing

How to Write Your First Novel

Save Your One Person Business From Extinction

Amazon Chap-Books:

How to Be Beautiful

How to Keep Calm and Carry On Without Money

TO ANY LENGTHS
A NOVEL

Jacqueline Gay Walley

PUBLICATIONS

Book Two of the VENUS AS SHE AGES *Collection*

I have lived many of the places I write about, many of these characters are based on real people, alive or dead, and I occasionally even use real names, so it is understandable people may think these are real stories. But this book is a work of fiction, because all the events and places are transmuted into a story that the real people would not recognize. That said, it bears repeating that nothing in the novel is intended as a recounting of actual events. Apart from the broad parallels, this is not what actually happened to me, nor to the people I write about.

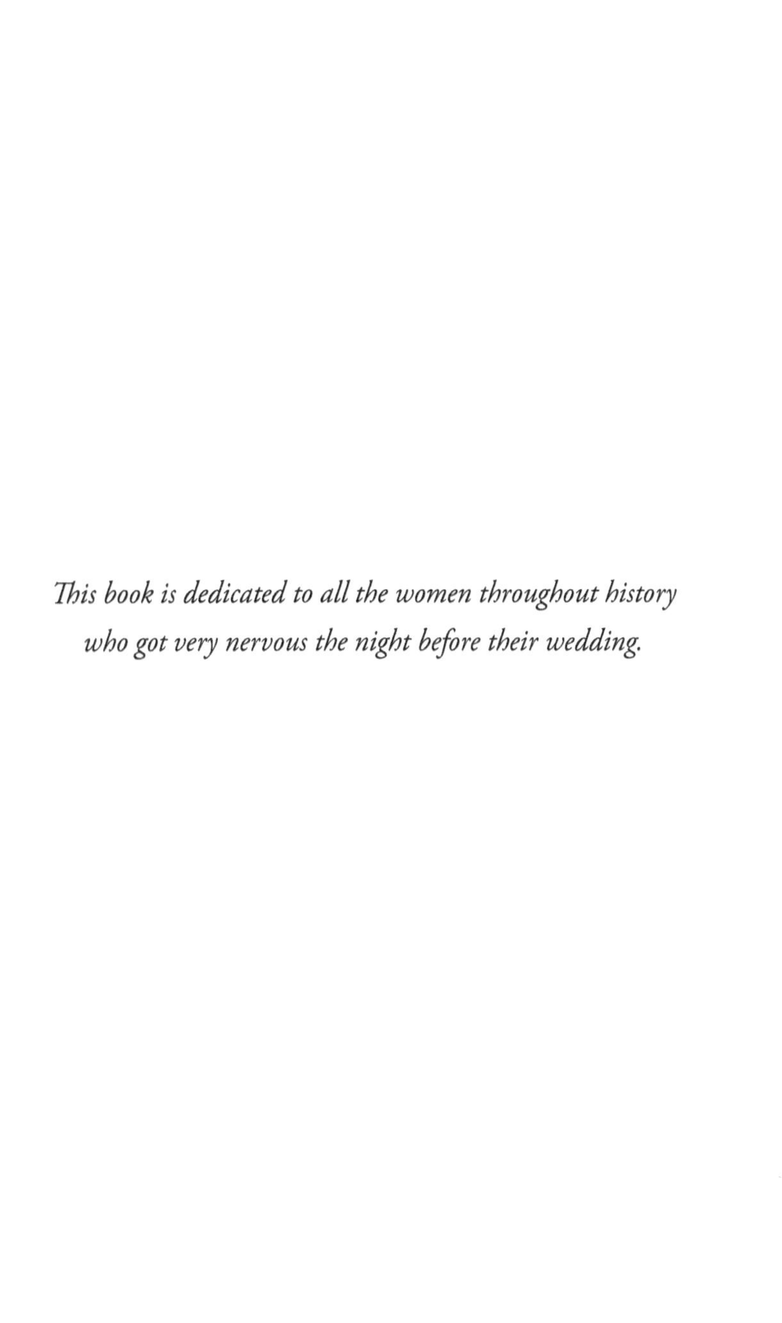

*This book is dedicated to all the women throughout history
who got very nervous the night before their wedding.*

PART ONE

CHAPTER 1

David tells me there's a whole group of men who read my stories. "They like them," he says, and then they ask him, "What's this broad look like?" He shows them my pictures. "They like your neck," he continues after he stops mid-sentence during our visit and looks down the cavern of my black velvet smock to the peak of my black lace bra. Then his eyes travel back up again and holds onto my neck for a moment and then he says, "Don't send Polaroids because the prison guards tear off the backs to look for hidden drugs so the two Polaroids you sent are kind of bad."

David tells me that my stories won't sell unless I give them a story. They're heady and psychological and he loves that, "Don't get me wrong," he says, but he doesn't know if he would continue reading if he wasn't reading them here. The guys and he prefer the stories with sex in them. And I make a point of sending the ones with sex in them; I know those are the ones they will read. "You have the hard part down," he says, "the psychological stuff. You just need a story. There are some amazing stories here," he says looking round.

"See that guy? He was in the Oliver North case. He's brilliant, a linguist. He gave a class in Shakespeare. Only 3 men, myself included, stuck it out."

I look at an older man with wire rim glasses in neat beige prison khakis. Mister Chips.

A dark haired guy with missing teeth and a big smile slaps David on the back as he walks by and then sits diagonally across from us with his smiling wife.

"That guy's a stand up guy," David says to me. "Took me aside the first day and said here's how you do time." David laughs to himself. "He's done 6 years now, goes to the hole quite a bit. Doesn't take any nonsense."

The dark haired guy is talking to his wife but his eyes look over at us.

"You're short now, aren't you?" David yells to him for my benefit.

 To Any Lengths

"Only 37 months," the man says. "Nothing to it."

David likes to laugh. Then he leans forward, "This place has to affect you," he says worriedly, "so I don't concentrate on the outside. Guys go crazy on the phone when they're trying to keep a woman or a business going on the outside. You can't if you're in for more than two years. You have to focus on doing the thing here. That way you have a chance."

It flashes through my mind that's the way you have a chance with anything but I don't say it.

He points to a new inmate whom he is fathering, he says, although they are the same age. The guy is having a hard time. He's already had his jaw broken once. I look over at this sandy haired man, with a neat beard and short ponytail. Close cropped curly hair, a man I find myself strangely attracted to. He is so intent on his conversation. It cons me into thinking he has untold stories. He is wearing the orange overalls of men who have not been assigned a permanent prison yet. David says he never stops talking about his case. He plea-bargained for twenty years and he will have to serve eighteen. David says he can't make the adjustment yet. He made a huge amount of money as a marijuana smuggler but David says the feds take everything. David mentions the Shah of Iran or someone as his client but I am not that big for name-dropping, at least not in prison. The man dressed in orange overalls never smiles as he talks to the floor while his friend listens but sometimes he looks up and catches my eye. This is what used to happen in bars when I was young. He was the kind of man I would end up with—the one who, covertly, across the room, caught my eye. I would misinterpret his worried intensity as the intensity with which he would love me. Usually it turned out the guy simply had a lot of problems.

David, on the other hand, is tall and handsome with eyes that never look at you unless he is working you. He has a way of making you feel as if you are being manhandled but very, very gently. He always had 3-4 girlfriends at once on the outside. I wouldn't put it past him having them now. His first wife was a famous rock star. He put his second wife through law school.

He says he wonders why we never got together on the outside, except for one night when we drank too much.

I don't remember the sex that night, and he doesn't either because he often turns to me and asks, "Tell me, did we do it?"

"Must have been incredibly memorable for you," I say.

"I must have been drunk is what it is."

I must have been closed down is what it was, for I knew he was a kid even then. We had gone dancing, and when we left the nightclub David smashed into several cars as he roared and lurched out of the parking lot, his tires screeching. He never

     To Any Lengths

stopped to reckon with the damage. That's when I decided not to fall in love with him. I could never trust someone so casual about his wake.

I look round the prison visiting room and notice that all these men look like kids. They're clean-shaven, smiling naughty boys who get caught.

"These guys have a lot of spirit," David says. "They're the ones who break the rules. You should hear the things they think they're going to do when they get out of here."

They're surprisingly fresh looking, I notice. They seem to preen themselves. Except David. He looks disheveled, hunted, being here.

"You shouldn't have had partners. That's what gets people caught," I say leaning in slightly toward him. "Partners."

"The operation was too big, I had to."

"I was too serious for you when we were young," I say, changing the subject. "Maybe not now." I look appraisingly at the tension in his eyes.

Earlier, while I was waiting for David, one of the inmates' mothers came over and began talking to me. Her son, she said, was the target of a sting. He's not guilty. And another mother touched my sleeve and said her son was just loaning out his garage. He had found the Bible here so that was something. She had been a Witness herself for 30 years.

Boys. The mothers visit vigilantly.

You can die in a Federal prison. Pick up the pool cue in anger because you booked the table to play and the men before you won't stop playing their game. There's not much else to do, maybe even for the next 7 or 100 years, so you just pick up a pool cue.

David and I share an ice cream and popcorn sitting on the locked down chairs.I already bought him plastic covered ravioli from the vending machine. He has to stand to the side of the vending machines and watch me press C2 or F6 for potato chips or Coca-Cola. They're not allowed to touch the vending machines, not allowed to handle money, these men, most of whom have touched more money than I probably ever will.

"I love your looks. I've never seen anyone who looks like you," he says. Last time I visited him he sent me a photo of Michelangelo's Venus (where did he get it, it must have been one of his treasures) and said it reminded him of me. No one says that to me on the outside.

"It's not only you're beautiful," he says, "but you have a spirit inside you that glows."

My boyfriend says, how can you spend money you don't have visiting him? Is that your priority? "You don't need to write in story form. Look at where you're getting your advice. You're taking literary criticism from prisoners for Christ's sake," and Jesus, there's a whole literary tradition around prisoners but that's another matter and usually a French one, and David and I think up a story during our visit where a prisoner steals a man's girlfriend solely by his wits. He can't offer her anything but his impeccable timing in his letters, phone calls, in guarded visits. In our story, his thievery of her affection goes as smoothly as a first time razor. She drops the boyfriend and falls in love with the prisoner. I am hoping our romantic convict dies in prison because does she really want to deal with him on the outside?

"Well why doesn't he like you visiting me?" David asks me.

"He says I can't afford it right now. I should be working."

"It'll come back to you," David says.

"I know."

"Anyway, I have some ideas," he says, "on how you could make money."

"David," I say, "I wouldn't be good as a criminal."

"Yeah you're right," he says. "You wouldn't."

"Oh?" I say offended. "Why not?"

"You always have more than one thing going on in your head at the same time. You're right there when you're with someone, I was explaining that to one of the guys. But other times, you're—I don't know—spacey." He laughs affectionately; after all he is a man who knows how to focus. Meanwhile I'm spacey and I'm the one renting a car to visit him HERE? He moves forward in his chair. "I don't want to say it," he says.

"Say what?"

"You know, about your boyfriend. It's not right."

"There's nothing you can say that hasn't been said before. Believe me."

"Well, you don't need someone constraining you. He's frightened of your freedom. You need encouragement. A writer needs encouragement."

I am sunning myself in those words, a blue and silver dolphin breaking the surface, encouragement that's what I need, when the guard calls out "Three o'clock." I look around and there is plenty of French kissing going on and daughters climbing up and cleaving desperately to their fathers' chests and shoulders while the guards get anxious to lock the prisoners, as they say, down. David walks me to the door of the visiting room. Kisses me but I don't respond passionately. That's for stories and not the kind I write. He says, "What if I make you my obsession?"

"Well getting through my defenses is harder than breaking out of here."

His eyes light up. "Really?"

I knew they would.

     To Any Lengths

"Oh yes," I say.

Then I twirl my big coat round my legs and know he is, as always, watching me as the guards lock us visitors in one room while waiting to unlock the doors to the next room where we wait while they unlock the doors of the next room till finally they herd us down a walkway, woman, child, mother and stool pigeon till we are free and luscious in the grey afternoon of the crowded parking lot.

CHAPTER 2

It's very thick and I can tell he's poured his heart out to me and I open the envelope ravenously while I run steaming water into the tub. I skim the letter while the water's pouring, throw it on the floor, save it for later, and answer another letter (on a wooden board that my boyfriend made so I can write in the tub) from a woman I don't even like, and then wet I rush to my bed—to an imaginary vision of my boyfriend and a beautiful exotic woman who opens her legs to a complete V to the sky when he comes, but it really is David and me, me as the beautiful exotic woman, he says I am exotic and he questioned me in the letter, he questioned why am I elusive emotionally with him, what boundary breaking could I possibly be frightened of, after all hadn't I noticed there are guards, razor wire, dogs, search lights, cameras and so on. He is right of course, he says he wants to retain his most primitive emotions, anger, desire, hunger and here you are, he says, why, why are you shutting them off?

As I walk, I say, well I don't want to open up with a prisoner for god's sake, even I can figure that one out, and I think about a healthy relationship for me, one where the guy is reasonable, financially sound, a professional, loyal, a good husband but while I'm doing this I see myself decorate my living room for David's welcome home party. In about 4 years. Will he like the trees from my bedroom window? What will he feel like to sleep next to? Will he hold me gently or will he jump quickly to other things after the initial claiming? I introduce him to all my friends at this imaginary party. I am not proprietary of him, he is a free man, but he loves me, he loves me because he knows me.

Anyway . . . Could a prisoner through his letters open me up faster and more artfully than my analyst who says, "Why do you need danger, excitement to love?"

"I need it creatively. Although not really. No, not anymore," I say, "I don't." I tell the analyst, "Well I didn't have relationships, as you keep calling them, when I was young. For instance my kind of relationship was one with a surrealist painter whose paintings were as stark and inhuman as his ability for affection. That painter said he liked to paint at night, contrary to what I'd heard other painters liked. Anyone that original must be worthy of me. Later I learned he painted at night because he entertained other people's wives during the day, and my slot was about four in the morning, while still dark, and he would steal into my bed, wake me making love, and then leave when I went to work."

"Purely sexual," my shrink says.

"Yes."

"Nothing wrong with that," he says. "You wanted those kind of relationships because you would not have to feel any longing, any rekindling of feelings that were traumatized in your childhood."

David may think in my stories I am the night watchman of psychology but he doesn't hear the shrink ask me, "Why do you keep tapping your fingers on the wall?"

The shrink keeps suggesting I have a sexual relationship (imaginary) with him. But I'm already having an imaginary relationship with a prisoner. How many do I need? The fact is David's letters are brilliant. You could say, in that department, in the area of sensitivity and romance, I have met my match.

My boyfriend says that he was the first one to tell me: you need a story. But I say that inside all those bruised grooves and dark secrets are so many stories, one has to wait for them to come up, in their own way, in their own divulging, in their own wisdom. David's letter is on my table. This morning my boyfriend begins reading it with a big smirk on his face. "Don't read my mail," I say, as I come out from the bath.

"You would give me a helluva an attitude if I was writing some female prisoner," he says. "If I was driving three hours to nowhere to see her."

"That's true. But I would let you know where I stand about it. I would show my jealousy," I say victoriously.

"I'm a bigger person than you are," he says.

After my boyfriend leaves, I sit in the tub and write David back. I have a long soak and take an hour to write him. I throw caution to the wind; I tell him that he has inspired my imagination, that he has given me back the woman clamoring, the woman banging at the bars. What can I give him I ask? Tell me in your next letter. I want to make love with him on the grass in the fenced-in tiny area outside the visiting room, have him slip in his desire and even better mine.

For some reason my letter includes the fact my mother has long crimson nails. I type, "My better has long crimson nails." A Freudian typo, it seems.

I have short pink nails.

I see stories everywhere.

David bringing a gun into my therapy room and standing at the door and asking me to leave right now, go with him to Montevideo. Choose, we'll live outside the law and never come back. I, who can never decide anything. I walk along the street and wonder, Would I go? No, not me. I tell him from the analyst's couch, Thanks, but no. Very kind of you to ask. You need someone younger. That was me in the past. I'm going to stay and work it out. Don't get caught now. Take care.

But in my fantasy he keeps asking over and over. I always get another chance.

I remember I mourned my father's death by dressing myself up as a gun moll and getting drunk in the local bars. I've been a mistress, working girl, sexual object, talking head, never committed, never a wife and mother. Now my boyfriend wants me to be a wife and mother and instead of giving him an answer I keep wondering what to say when the prisoner finally breaks into my therapy group and says, "We've gotta go now."

"What did you say?" I ask.

The shrink says, "Daddy."

Fuck you and the gun you came in on.

CHAPTER 3

"Why don't you have a mock marriage with your boyfriend?" my shrink suggests. "Rather than live with him for another six months, marry him, and if you are unhappy, then divorce him. That's one way to decide if you want to stay together. You've been in this dilemma of whether to marry him for so long. How long is it?"

"Ten years," I say. "Marry him for a short time? It's creative, I'll give you that."

The shrink says he was a rebel when young and this is how he channels it, into creativity.

"You could stick with the marriage if you like it," he says.

It was such a freeing thought in a way, just do it, throw all caution to the wind. I can recover if it is a drastic mistake. After all, people do.

I would get to stop thinking about it.

"You'll be more desirable," he says, "as a divorcee than as a spinster."

Then the shrink said that I must not turn myself so against myself. That if I am kind to myself, supportive, encouraging, patient, believe in myself, if I encourage myself with kindness and understanding, then I will blossom in my story telling, in my ability to withstand intimacy. "Undoubtedly," I say.

What a thought.

I walk home in the sun, feeling safe.

And then, like an idiot, I call my mother to tell her I am coming to Montreal to visit, as promised. Our bi-annual day and a half visit where I count the minutes until I board the plane back.

"Let's rent a car and visit the mountains together," I say creatively to her on the phone. Let's try something new. Perhaps I could enjoy this visit to the so-called living parent. She of the dyed red hair and the deadening stories of how brilliant she is, how everyone admires her, how many, many men loved her. None of these stories, even if they are true, seem to be so if they need this much repetition.

   To Any Lengths

I hate the thought of sitting for days in her apartment, discussing her past affairs and how to make my affairs things of the past. That is what we do.

It was my father I adored. My father who took me away from her when I was four. Or who was left with me. I'll never know exactly since he is dead and she lies. He lied too when he was alive, but I listened more closely to him and could deduce some truth from several cross-examinations.

Sometimes I tell myself he took me away because she was dangerous. He knew she was a potential child murderer and didn't want to leave me with her. He was too British to ever come out and say this kind of thing to me. Although he had no problem telling me she was a whore, liar, and totally disgusting so why I think he would blanch at telling me she was a child murderer I don't know. Other times, I feel she just walked out because she didn't want the responsibility. The responsibility of loving might bring out the murderer in her. Or maybe the fact she didn't love her child might bring out the murderer in me. Anyway I don't know the truth and I suspect it is not that interesting. She just left. Thankfully, it could not have been any other way.

"Absolutely not. I don't want to go on any trip to the mountains," she replies. "What do you need to be bored round these silly Laurentians?"

"I like them. It's pretty boring sitting around your apartment."

"No. I am not doing it," she says. "That's final."

There it is. Who needs the middle chapters?

Today she called to cancel my visit altogether. She has some event that Saturday night, she forgot, and then there is the hairdresser. But really, she is angry about the conversation the day before. I should want to sit in an apartment with her and hear her stories. Not spend thousands of dollars renting a car.

Thousands of dollars for one day?

"You don't know what the taxes are like here. You don't mind spending thousands of dollars with a psychoanalyst because you are so hostile."

"Hostile? This is hostile. And why do you think I see an analyst?"

"I met him. He never said it was my fault."

Her one visit and she insisted on going with me to see him. She crossed her legs prettily and began of course a course about herself.

"You're very vivacious," the shrink said to her.

"The worst thing," she said to him, "must be having to see people who are boring. I couldn't take that," she said, "I would hate to have to see boring people. I am not boring, you have to admit that," she said.

Nothing is more boring than her stories. Maybe that is why I am suspicious of stories. Her stories that shut off my entire breathing apparatus.

"I'm not getting tricked into discussing whose fault is whose," I said on the phone and then, unfortunately, I had a system shut down.

Then she said, "The weather is bad in Montreal, terrible." What does she want me to do? Commiserate? I don't want to mother my mother, not when she never mothered me. They said I screamed when passed to her as a baby. I am convinced she tried to kill me because why else would I choose to open up with a man safely behind bars. My father said she never even changed us. He had to. She hated our little vulnerable bodies. I screamed when passed to her.

The last time I remember asking her for anything, a glass of milk, I was six. She was sitting at a kitchen table, visiting my father, maybe to discuss a possible reconciliation or how she was abandoned by some lover at the time. Maybe my father was her father confessor, a British drunk more than 20 years older than her refugee Viennese self. I interrupted her sitting alone at the kitchen table. She must have been waiting for him or maybe they had already spoken. She was crying. I wanted some milk. I plucked up my courage and soon found myself falling down a steep flight of stairs. I learned not to ask again. I became a quiet child. I spent other nights in hospital, as a small child, but no one remembers why. Bad dreams, I thought as a four-year-old. I was frightened to go to sleep because my dreams were so bad. That's why they put me in hospital.

I don't remember more about my mother and her young mothering. But you do see why I was ecstatic she left.

Thirty-six years later I ask for a mutual drive in the country . . .

She said I should be kind to her because she will leave me money.

"I don't want to be blackmailed about your will."

I told my father, when I was four, maybe 3 or 4 days before she left, I sat at her dressing table while he was dressing and I said, "Get rid of her. She's a witch. Dangerous."

He laughed. "Don't worry about her. It'll all work out. Perhaps you're right," he said, "and she is a witch."

The next week she was gone.

Today I received a postcard from David. It was a self-portrait by Frida Kahlo of her sitting with four lush parrots, 2 on her shoulders, 2 at her breasts. Her long black eyebrows meet above her nose, her hand holds a cigarette. She looks like she is facing it down. He thanks me for coming, appreciates the turmoil, as he puts it, I submit myself to, coming on these visits. They mean a lot to him and so do I I'm a treat and well yes he might be a bit like Byron the Byron of Fairton Correctional Institute as I named him but he would throw in a bit of Bukowski he's got a work proposition for me. Much Love, David.

My boyfriend, I notice, signs his notes or cards to me Love Always or he signs Always. I am charmed but frightened by my boyfriend's salutations. They smack of irrevocableness. Much Love as in David sounds free.

David of the wide chest and big arms. Push-ups that only a criminal would subject himself to or someone very vain. David of the light laughter. The other prisoners' little girls come smiling up to him in the visiting room with their coloring books and puzzles and he says gently "What you got there baby?" and these little four year olds twist around at his knee and lift way-too-mature doleful eyes at him. He needs glasses to see what they got there. He didn't bring them when he came out to see me. I saw him comb his hair through the tiny window before they unlocked the door for him to come out to see me. I wondered if, at a certain angle, I could see the strip searches.

"Read what you wrote him," I say to the little girls.

But the little girls darkly make a point of not looking at me. They just look up at David. One of them fondles and twists her doll necklace hanging round her neck. David asks if the doll has a name. "Jewel," she says shyly and runs off. "It's name is Jewel."

He looks at me and laughs.

But I am smacked by these children's refusal of me. They want me out of the picture. Their desire for this is violent, let's face it.

That little girl with the necklace at his knee, well, you just met my mother.

CHAPTER 4

David sent me an early poem of Ezra Pound's, The Virginal, where Pound expounds his admiration for a delicate woman. David says she reminds him of me. He says he does imitations for the men of how delicately I bend down to pick up change I drop at the vending machine. It's true; I am always dropping things when I am there. I get embarrassed at how he watches me so carefully, as if he is memorizing me.

I sent some writing to him and the guys, a $20 postal money order, and a copy of two paintings for his cell. And I slipped in that I am considering marrying my boyfriend. I told him that he should be glad I am not HIS since my insecurities are incessant;

I need constant soothing like a baby.

He says he is writing me a treatise on marriage. Even though he has been married twice, he is against it and here is where I better watch it, getting marital advice from a prisoner. Bad enough the extent of literary stimulus I am divining from him.

Today I'll tell you a story. About an average-sized and shaped woman, at what now would be considered an average age, 41. Forty-one is no longer old if you're endowed with a healthy vanity, which I am, for I am loath to relinquish any power. I am not at full throttle in that department, not a vibrating woman in her twenties. When I'm tired I can make you tired just by looking at me, but I have retained a lived-in look, a cinematic face so I command a certain attention. Not a sexual attention but I am willing to forfeit that because really where did it get me? It was all so hurried, pressing, people hungering to get to bed and none of it much to do with me. Now to be left in the peace of being a woman to be reckoned with and perhaps to be slept with is much more appealing.

I have not married and had children and indeed, as you know, have a younger boyfriend who presses me to do so. He must still see me as he met me when I was 31, on the seashore, a catch at the time, willful, sophisticated for I harken from those

       To Any Lengths

European parents I have told you of, and this in a small American fishing town was rather outstanding and he wanted much to be outstanding for his father had been a famous poet.

I rescued the son from that small town, took him with me to large cities, variant work, films, plays and music. These I dragged him to till he was well exhausted with it and perhaps hankered for the simplicity of those wooden brass bars he had met me in where conversation leaned to what the sea level was that day, who was building what boat and who had recently applied for unemployment. But by the time he realized he missed his former world, he had learned its limitations. So, he became a Knut Hamsun character, odd in his yellow suit, an intellectual to carpenters, a natural man to intellectuals.

And I do love him, no matter what I say. Not for his mind, for he huffs and puffs his greatness to his dead poet father in the sky and the very huffing and puffing I find distracting, isn't greatness wry and self-effacing, but I love his desire for greatness and his having even known it and his ensuing fidelity to truth. He is a poet's son in his not even being tempted to work as a salesman, or on the stock exchange, in his belief in selfishness. He would never tell a lie. He does not have to.

My boyfriend, I am sure, wonders what he is doing with this woman who spends most of her time contradicting herself, but

I think it is that he has fun with me. I am game for every walk, drive, dinner, breakfast and not much gets me down since so much did so early.

As you can see, I don't want to go into the details of my early life. Although people say that is the real material. But why should it be?

Thank God I have always loved to hide myself in work, any kind of work. Everyone complains about it but work is healthy, constructive. Writing stories does not feel that way and it occurs to me that that might be because I do not work at it.

But I wonder, Do people marry to avoid feelings of worthlessness if they are not connected to someone? That will be my reason, I can tell you now.

CHAPTER 5

"You know I love you darling. We must have done something pretty right to have you come out so well."

This is the kind of thing my mother says.

And my shrink asks me why I can't take a compliment.

CHAPTER 6

My boyfriend and I got the marriage intention license yesterday. We stood at the wooden counter of the sea town's City Hall and filled in our parents' names, our own names, where and when we were born. Then I had to put down if I was taking his name.

"I don't know what to do," I say to him.

"Oh come on, do it."

I check yes to make him happy, after all this is all for him anyway, but does this mean that I will be checking yes to all kinds of things, once we're married. Will I become a thing of the past?

He smiles happily to the short woman behind the counter at this rare display of acquiescence on my part. A good sign of

 To Any Lengths

things to come.

The lady who works in City Hall smiles back daftly and sentimentally at this parody of our being a pleasant about-to-be-wedded couple. I find myself strangely enjoying this play I am appearing in. I had never imagined myself in such a part and there is a pleasure, a wonderful pleasure, when life delivers you the unexpected. I look behind the desk into her "area" and see rows upon rows of file cabinets full of what I deem to be marriage intention licenses. I will now be in a file cabinet.

Can I survive? I remind myself my intended is the kind of man to take me places so remote the motels have long ago turned off the heat.He is the kind of man who never knows where to take me on my birthday. He assumes I won't like his choice and there is some truth to that.

It will not be a life where I catch myself smiling. I might have to beg and scream for happiness.

We are now standing outside on the City Hall steps. I can hear the seagulls by the fishing boats behind the buildings. My boyfriend is tall and handsome and amazed he has pulled off this coup. Progress with the recalcitrant me.

"Remind me again. Why are we getting married?" I ask, just to torture him.

"For security. I'll be less angry. You'll see."

"But you don't even like me."

He puts his arm around me. "I like you," he says, "sometimes. I just want you to be different."

He is joking and not joking. Just like I am about marriage.

"Well, I'm still debating," I say.

"We'll be married twenty years and you'll still be making up your mind."

I lean up and kiss his neck, happy. I love his neck, which is strong. I love touching him. His body is hard and long and somehow because I can never get close enough to it, I am always desiring him. Is he aware of this sadomasochism between us?

He pushes me away, as always, when I initiate intimacy. I am forced to return to myself.

We begin walking to the car and I tell myself, as we walk holding hands, that I have a week before the invitations go out. I am conventional enough to think, once they're out, I'm in.

We now drive to the place where he always takes a sauna when we are visiting his sea-town. If I peak round the corner, I see lots of naked men coming in and out of the little building where they happily sweat nakedly together.

I decide to wait for him under a tree. The wind should be blowing the bugs away but it isn't. I move to another patch of grass to get away from the bugs. I watch the man who owns the

    To Any Lengths

sauna parade around on his motorized garden cart, his wife close by with her clippers. Would that I could live so peaceably.

David's family home is only one quarry over but I have never been there. There is a road named after his family. I think of him in jail and my heart slinks deeper into my chest.

Last Saturday I visited him. It was our most difficult visit yet. I dressed early in the morning, it was just past sunrise when I left. I was tired, an old friend who was visiting me was sleeping in my bedroom and I did not want to wake her, so blindly I grabbed a black t-shirt, a flowered skirt.

David told me to dress sexy.

I said, "That's ridiculous when visiting a prison."

"You should see how the Spanish women come in here," he said.

"I'm not Spanish."

Still when I arrived at the prison, after getting lost, a long 3-hour drive that wore me out, after all it was a Saturday, a pretty one, I just wanted to go in, do my good deed, then go back to my friend and a planned night at the theatre.

 No you can't have a locker. Leave your handbag and book in the car. Leave your lipstick at the front desk. Change goes inside a clear plastic bag. We're not finished yet, Miss. A woman guard motions to me. "I can't let you in." Some insurrection of

David's I'm thinking.

"Why not?"

"The way you're dressed," she said. "You have no brassiere on."

"Well isn't there a rule book for visitors to follow? I have just driven 3 hours. I didn't know there's a dress code."

She began giving me elaborate directions to a Kmart 10 miles away so I could buy a bra. As I listened, I saw an eleven-year-old Black girl holding her jean jacket, waiting to be called in with her family. I turn from the guard and walk to the little girl's unsmiling guardians.

"Can I borrow that jacket? The guards won't let me in without one. I'll leave with you if you are leaving early, I just drove from New York."

The grandmother says coldly, "It's my granddaughter's . . ." and then a handsome tall Black man says, "Let her take it" and I negotiate with him when to return it. The little girl in pink ribbon pigtails flashes me a beautiful smile when I mouth a private thank you from the prison guard's desk.

This prison guard woman still does not like me. She waits a long time to call me, long after the others who came in with and after me have gone in. Usually timid, I march to the desk. I argue. Finally I get through. Prison wives wait patiently, old hands, and look dispassionately at this white woman who doesn't

     To Any Lengths

know what the hell she's doing with herself.

David is late too and when he finally comes out, he is not faring much better. He begins a story of being held up, strip-searched. He was wearing the wrong shoes. His guard gave him the You Can't Go In speech too. "She has driven 3 hours and I have to change my shoes?"

He changed his shoes.

David greets me, his eyes flying wildly. "It's the pettiness," he says, "that kills you. I almost got thrown into the hole. I could have punched the guard I was so angry."

"Thank God you didn't," I say, taking his arm. This visit I don't take my arm off him. And I am glad because later when I ask him what's it like for all these guys living without women, I ask this as I stare at Gotti's driver with his patched up face, then at another young man who may get lethal injection for a murder indictment, a witness saw him throw the body into the river and I am deliberating whom do I feel sorry for, the person in the river or this young guy whose eyes I can actually see facing death, I feel sorry for all of us, I realize, and then I hear David saying that men talk about missing sex but you can have sex by yourself. "What they really miss is the touching, tenderness. You can't make it here without some tenderness and touching," he says.

I keep my arm on him all the time. I hold his hand as we

walk through the visiting room to the tiny fenced-in prison yard. I look out at the thinly planted trees beyond the fence. We stand in the sun, our arms around each other's waists. A guard comes and tells us to separate. Can't do that. I had forgotten where we were, wrapped close in the sun.

I know what he means about this being touched business. It is why I might go to prison, too. I need the warmth, the assurance of my intended's body. I don't want a life where there are no arms around me. I need the volumes in another's pores. That is what David says the men miss and never did I feel we were more well suited.

He was particularly intense that visit. I was encouraging but his dark mood didn't lift. Prison is getting to him. He urges me to send black and white photos so he can draw me. They will not let him sculpt.I tell him my friend staying with me loved his photo. I tell him maybe if I show his photo to enough women, they will form a liberation army, in high heels, no less. I tell him I will have a waiting line of women at his coming out party. I tell him all this to cheer him.

One of the prisoners interrupts us and asks if I am a model. The guy in orange overalls from the time before, the one I liked. The one having a hard time. He wants to talk. I look to David as if we should be kind and invite him into our house for tea

 To Any Lengths

but David is annoyed and pays his friend no attention. Cons everywhere. I smile and shrug coquettishly, back in the bar again. The prisoner leaves, encouraged.

David asks about my father. I spend 3 minutes on a response, I don't want to talk about my father, I need energy for that, it is painful because he is dead and I loved him so, but even a three-minute description gives over, inescapably, that my father was a renegade. His three marriages made up of true love for barmaids, house building one day credit card evacuation the next, his hiding his passport, driver's license, birth certificate in the trunk of his car so no one would know his age so he could start all over again in work and love, his moving from country to country. The odd man out whom I supported in being the odd man out.I am not surprised I am here. My father never wanted the normal life.

David tells me I am the right size for him. How did I get so good looking? He says he will not be a playboy when he gets out. Hah, I say. He wants to share a loft in New York, with lots of space to do our respective work. I don't tell him I hate lofts. They are passé.

He says I seem chipper and he thinks it is because I am off the hook for the marriage. He's right in a way. My boyfriend has been so crazy since I agreed to marry him that no one sane would go ahead and marry this kind of contradictory behavior. All of a sudden my boyfriend wants to leave New York. We'll just live, he suggests, wherever the car breaks down. I haven't done that kind of thing since I was seventeen and I didn't even do it then. Money, he says, is not a priority. I agree but the need for it is.

"Well," I say for no apparent reason, "my boyfriend wants children."

David looks at me and says, "Children are great, don't get me wrong, but a lot of it is mundane."

How does he know I wonder about that?

I still don't kiss him passionately, I won't give myself to him, when we say goodbye but as he says in his letters it is getting harder to say goodbye. This week I got a post-visit love letter. Where he describes my beauty and intelligence, in original terms, where he tells me how I make him forget prison. I write him back immediately, from my tub, I tell him he is making love to me with these eloquent letters of admiration. I tell him I feel much for him too but what I feel goes into my story and that is the dread of being involved with a writer. He says I need spontaneity and that is a deadly combination for him and that is the first hint I get that something could go awry in this love story that is constrained in my favor.

So I was in a veritable maze of mental lovemaking when my

 To Any Lengths

intended and I went to visit mutual friends who know David. At their elegant dinner table, candles burning, food overflowing, the husband inexplicably began complaining that he and his wife don't have enough sex.

"She doesn't even like sex," the husband said.

I look at my boyfriend and raise my eyebrows to say We Don't Even Know These People That Well. Then I turn to the wife in hopes of a catfight.

"You're right," the wife said, "I don't like sex."

I said, "How about the touching? Do you like the touching, the tenderness?"

And then it occurred to me that I am sensual, what with my passion for the sun, my passion for men's faces and bodies, for hot water. Perhaps I am not a horrible woman.

"Do I like the tenderness?" she asks herself out loud,

"No."

"Well," I say, "you know, I saw David—in prison—and he said that the men there—"

Suddenly this husband and wife began screaming in unison at me.

The husband, "WHY DO YOU SEE HIM? HIM OF ALL PEOPLE?"

The wife, "WHAT IF DAVID'S WIFE KNEW YOU VISIT

HIM?"

I blush—has he lied to me and is still married? No, she says but they are sure to go back together. They were together 15 years. Oh how beautiful, she goes on, is David's wife. And how could he leave her with that little girl how could he be so irresponsible and yes I agree they will go back together, he deserves to be with a beautiful wife, and then this woman pulls out photographs of David's wife, for they were in a mother's group together and there is David's wife, pretty and smiling with their little girl and I think Jesus what am I doing?

I was only being compassionate, he's nearby, but would

I visit this woman's husband if he was in prison? He wouldn't add the bonus of making love to me. He doesn't walk any dangerous lines.

The husband yells again, "WHY DO YOU GO THERE?"

My boyfriend finally speaks up: "To Break my Balls."

The wife begins again, "How could he have treated her so terribly? He's very attractive to women, handsome and attentive, he knows just what to say to make a woman putty in his hands. It's just terrible."

Terrible how? Terrible that her own husband says that seeing women from his car when he is driving, in elevators, in restaurants, is more than he can take, he is so full of desire to break out.

Yet I have been unmasked. My boyfriend says nothing. The subject gets dropped and on we go from bad to worse. What is wrong with you, the couple yell at me, to have put off this goddamn marriage after is it 11 years now it can't be it is Jesus Charlie how can you stand it?

And I look over at him and he doesn't look like he is standing it at all.

CHAPTER 7

I will try to describe my boyfriend so you can see him clearly. I am going to do it in a convoluted way.

I was thinking about my boyfriend, trying to get a fix on his personality and I found myself doing it by comparison. Autodidacts and savages learn what's right and wrong by watching how the other people do it.

Last night I met another man my boyfriend's age, 37. This other man and I sat on a couch at a party given by a woman I work for. Personal trainers, pleasure boat sailors, insurance agents, friendly maintenance men and some other weaklings like myself who make money off this woman comprised the guest list. This particular man I am telling you of wore glasses so I gave him some points for possible introspection and indeed he did turn out to be able to hold a conversation, something I was having difficulty with the other guests, so busy were they on health clubs and industrial design marketing.

The guy in question was a successful pension fund manager, he had been educated etcetera, etcetera even lived in Europe and he wore exquisite shoes. Anyway this man had just split up with his wife and was in the throes of having to talk about it continuously and this was far more interesting to me than what kind of boats people were racing next week. He spoke about his having tried everything to make the marriage work, even seeing doctors as he put it, which I assumed to mean shrinks. He believes in taking risks, he said, and I couldn't quite follow the ensuing inspirational speech given for my benefit (did I look so sad?) But I liked him because I could see he was vulnerable.

"Well what was your wife like?" I asked.

Well she didn't vote; she only had a superficial knowledge of wines not liking to linger over, savor and discuss them as he did; she liked great restaurants only superficially; she really wasn't as interested in sailing as he was and if he could do it again he wouldn't have sailed as much yet sailing was not a necessity in a woman no it wasn't so I asked quickly, to cut this litany short,

"You mean she wasn't really a soul mate? Because all these things are . . ." and here I sort of mumbled "superficial" which he didn't hear me exactly mouth because he had brightened up so much at my observation.

"No that's right she wasn't a soul mate," he repeated.

Thus he was my friend for the night. (But not enough I noticed to give me a lift home so I could save $20 on a taxi. Finally he did offer but only after I had called for a taxi and perhaps this tells more about his married style than all the mannered conversation we had on the couch.)

Anyway my boyfriend is 37 also. In the cab I thought what would I think if I had just met my boyfriend on that couch. I don't think he would have been as generous in his conversation. His ideas when expressed would have seemed almost foreign in their stressed pedanticness. What IS the weather like in Guatemala this time of year? He would have spoken more loudly than this pension fund manager, booming out castigations against capitalism, his poet father's selfishness and so on to explain his not making his own business profitable. The other guy had enough successes under his belt financially, (and maybe a pair of rich loving parents to boot) to own some variant failures.

My boyfriend would have been more sexual, though, looking at me furtively and taking me in. He would compensate for the befuddlement in my piercing dark eyes at what he was saying by giving off a sexual emittance, which I am sure I would have preferred to that young Republican's articulate ravings. My boyfriend would be more guarded. He might have listened better than this young guy did, but only for passivity's sake.

My boyfriend would have laughed more I think but inappropriately, at things he would have said that made no sense to me and his laugh would be to obfuscate his and my confusion and I would have politely, coquettishly, laughed along with him. My boyfriend definitely would have offered me a lift and insisted I not call the taxi.Because he too would have wanted to get out of that sailing and marketing crowd party and $20 on a taxi would be a travesty to him. On the drive home, he would have discussed geography and the kind of car he was driving with me. Which I would not have in the least been interested in but I would have been interested in the kind of upright arcaneness of this young man discussing the Rio Grande Gorge as if it had just been discovered and I would have been (and am) impressed that he isn't the type to ever open up with self esteem and how to get it.

My boyfriend always seemed an original to me. Kind, a little out of touch.

I asked the young man last night, "Would you have to have a child in a relationship?" My boyfriend HAS to. No, this guy wouldn't.

My boyfriend wants to HAVE things—a child, wife, land. He goes about it in the most bizarre way, however, one foot on the gas pedal one on the brake, marrying a woman almost past childbearing age and very incredulous about her ability to rein in. He wants to marry a woman who just can't quite put her arms around the point of it and he wants land land more land but he hates the outrage of a system making monthly demands of him.

I find his "want" list quaint and especially so because he wants to include me in on it and no one, to be frank, wanted to include me in on much—I've always travelled solo, even as a child. My father's drunkenness left me to make all my own decisions, hence some very bad ones. I clung to false securities, jobs, boyfriends, drink, all enormous wasters of time, to distract me from the mountains of human kindness I hadn't known and now I'm sort of at 41 thinking all of it was false and terribly useless. None of it was transformative. Those visionaries like Kerouac, London and Jesus were right, you can't have one foot in the safety box and the other trying to dance itself up the road. You have to get fully out on the road, as K said, or as the Buddhists put it. Walk, walk; Run, run; But don't wobble. So the types of boyfriends, jobs, drinks that I conjured up to protect me simply kept me from living a life I might really enjoy. My boyfriend in his oom

     To Any Lengths

pa pa way knows that . . . Knows that you have to take the risk of a life that you care about. In his case he wants marriage a child commitment.

He pulls hard at my mismatched feet. "Move one for god's sake," he yells at me. "Make your feet both do the same thing. Marry me and get in. Or get out."

I want to, I really do. But what is this obscure calling calling me so obscurely that keeps whispering there is something else for me.

CHAPTER 8

The Buddhist koan: Hide yourself in the middle of the flames.

CHAPTER 9

Many things are peculiar about my mother and one of them is how she never remembers anything about me. Not the time I was born, not who my friends are, not what I do for a living. As a child, she shocked me with how she never could remember my age, what grade I was in, when school holidays started. Now, because in her mind I am approaching 50, she takes great pleasure in remembering my age. She brings up how old I am, how very old I am, over and over.

Sunday morning of the visit we eventually did have, the day I was to leave, she stayed in bed. She refused to go to lunch with me.

"No restaurants are open in Montreal today," she said.

It was beneath me to argue.

Thus I hung about anxiously, flipping through her back issues of Cosmopolitans and Vogues till finally I knew she would get dressed. Designer clothes, jewelry, makeup, and at my insistence we took a parting walk.

"It's such a beautiful Spring day," I said.

She selected a depressed shopping plaza to walk through, not the outdoors. "That's everywhere," she said. But only the very forlorn were inside that empty dark underground shopping plaza on that bright Canadian Spring day bursting forth from a long Canadian winter. Only the very angry would eschew that fulsome a Spring day to stay inside a mostly closed up shopping plaza.

Woolworth was open, I noted. I sneered painfully at the empty hot dog kiosks we passed. At least, my father would have taken me to the Ritz bar.

We each became exhausted with the harsh reality of being forced to be with one other for so long (day two), that I took a taxi to the airport early, as she had planned, and read an entire book in the bar, watching family members tease and well wish each other in Spanish Italian French and English. I watched alcoholic men carefully study their beer bottles while their neatly dressed wives pretended interest in planes docked at gates while fingering their gold necklaces. I watched them give their husbands an occasional

     TO ANY LENGTHS

indulgent smile for a news report on the beer bottle copy. Men with baseball caps covering baldness. Fat men reading paperbacks.

I read my own book, aptly named Solitude, and waited to go through customs. I did not drink, as I used to, but ate sugared blueberry yogurt.

I was back where I always go to recover. In a public place, pinpricking myself on how is it mothers love their children, what is it they do. I took solace in my expertise, the loneliness of alcoholic men.

No restaurants open in the entire city of Montreal, she said.

The first night we talked, she thought it was a mistake to marry my boyfriend. "You are the type," she said, "who would never leave."

Is marriage designed to be left? I wondered.

"You have too much guilt," she said. "I, I have no guilt. It is an odd thing about myself, I never had guilt. My parents," she said, "must have given me that."

"I can leave anyone," she said.

She forgets that her last two husbands left her. Not for younger women, she tells people who ask, but for nicer ones. I don't doubt it.

They left her. Correction number one. When they did leave, as if on cue, she would try, note "try," suicide and meet another man at the hospital or the spa she was recovering in. He would be married and here we begin again.

She did leave me, though, that is true.

"Amazing isn't it," she said, "how life works."

"They made it easy," I said. "Your men left you."

"Well maybe," she shrugged her shoulders.

I told my boyfriend I had conditions for marriage. He must get us health insurance, he must earn a steady income, he must take me on a date once a week.

He said I must not threaten to leave all the time. He is sick of it. That was his condition.

"Aren't you too old to have a child?" my mother asks.

"Yes, but it doesn't get through his head."

"Well you have 2 years maybe," she says, "what's the hurry? But if you had wanted to marry him, you would have done it by now."

I listen.

"If you had talent, you would have been published by 24."

I listen.

"You got something from your father," she offers me. "You got his class."

Over and over she said that.

Was she telling me I got something, and it didn't come from her?

     To Any Lengths

CHAPTER 10

This morning there is a message on my phone machine. Rambo of Fairton. David must be getting into fights. He no longer calls himself Byron of Fairton.

David calls again. He said Rimbaud not Rambo on the phone. I must be tired. He calls twice last night and warns me that marriage is quicksand; you can't get out once you're in. He tells me he is waiting for me, even if he is in prison. "I'm here," he says, "but we cannot get together if you are married. That doesn't work," he says and I am surprised he says that knowing how seriously he took his own and others' conjugal rights, he of the three changes of clothes in his car.

"I've gained different priorities in prison," he says. He would not want a woman who does not engage him mentally anymore and indeed, when I think about it, his wives have been intelligent.

It's his mistresses who tended to brain fluff and blonde hair.

"Why do you keep telling me I'm going to go back with my wife? It's over. I don't look back," he says.

He says he can handle anything if he can see clearly and he can see it all clearly now. I hold the phone totally befogged. He hasn't written me because he's been in the legal library trying to help a buddy with his case. A bomber, he says. David sounds as if he is enjoying himself in there. He calls me twice in the same night, a privilege; he knows how to get around the system. But we get off the phone before the second 10-minute allotment is up because the guards call for a massive lock down, a big fight between the inmates. I can hear animal yelling in the background.

If men had all their feelings, my shrink says, they would kill each other.

I am excited when I get off the phone.

David tells me not to get down about my writing rejections. When he was in Cambodia and everyone in his platoon except himself was killed, he didn't get down. He kept going he said. It was weird.

     TO ANY LENGTHS

Yet he puts himself in prison twenty years later. I am sure there is a corollary.

I loved David last night. I loved his perseverance through anything.

He said, "When's the bridal shower?"

I said, "I'm holding it at the Fairton Correctional Institute." I asked him if he is coming to my wedding. He said, "Why are you doing it if you don't want to."

"Get rid of that shrink," he says. "A six months marriage? You'll never get divorced."

"I'll be divorced by the time you get out."

David says, "Don't give me that stuff about you need soothing and security, you don't need it—"

But David, I don't say, you're forgetting the madwoman puts you in prison eventually, a fast thrilling erotic drive to prison—

Oh no it doesn't. I can hear him. It's the only way to get free.Dance, baby.

While meanwhile the prosaic turtle trudges along toward a slower, more banal—

He finishes the sentence: Vacuum.

Me: If you have peace, you can dream in safety of fire and mayhem. Fire and mayhem burn.

He: Jesus don't you want to burn? You're the one who wrote

hide yourself in the middle of the flames.

Me: Yes but safely. Sanely.

He: Give everything up and just feel.

Me: It sounds impractical.

He: It's more impractical to waste your life. Jesus, anybody can see what you really want is to be yourself. You'll be crazy till you finally do it.

Listen, I tell myself, everyone needs a defiant erotic fighting revolutionary solitary outspoken prisoner to mirror themselves to.

CHAPTER 11

My boyfriend and I are walking through Union Square prowling on a summer night. We do what all self-respecting tigers do, we fight. I, the female predator, am on the attack. I must run him off. Doesn't he know how dangerous I am? I love him and what I do is be as mean as I can be so he will leave me and live happily ever after.

After all, there is no happily ever after with me. I have never lived happily with me.

Here is where we are.

"I'm not giving you any plan about how I'm going to make money so we can get married," my boyfriend yells at me on the street. "My father's philosophy, his whole life work was against that kind of thing—he was a poet for chrissake—"

"Oh right. Let's recreate your family. Why don't you marry a woman like your mother? A student who gets knocked up and then is so depressed at the great poet, drinking with and writing letters to other women while she sits in an unheated apartment with her little son till she gets herself hit by a car. Let's recreate that. Go do it. Go find that woman."

That should do it. That should make him go and then I will grieve, as I am destined to, the rest of my life.

He walks off, very understandably.

I follow him across Eighteenth.

"I don't want to get stuck in a small life just so you can feel big. I just want to have a real conversation with you. Your mother didn't create any art in that artistic life of eating baloney and taking handouts. You think that's free? She gave up the piano. She gave it away to your father. Whatever her reasons were. You can't live an unconscious life happily."

He glares at me.

Then he turns a long hurt wounded face to me.

"Don't pull that," I say. "I know you had a hard childhood but it's time to grow up. It's over now. Daddy and Mommy hurt poor Charlie. It's time to grow up."

"Don't exhaust yourself," he says.

"Fuck you."

Silence.

"Alright, alright," I say, "I'm too much for you. You want someone younger who can do this without putting any thought into it go ahead you're free—"

"What do you mean?"

"You don't want to hear what I say so go ahead. Find this person who accepts you on any terms."

If only I could be that person. If only I could surrender. I want to. I want to be the other woman, the nice woman who surrenders, not the riven woman I am.

He must leave me.

It is the only way he will be safe.

I sit down on cold black iron stairs next to a closed-up shop with grates on the window. I feel the heat from the nearby subway grate opening. He keeps standing, a thin tree, looking up at the night sky.

"Okay," I say, "let's go have a coffee. We'll try and talk."

In single file we walk to a coffee shop. We can't leave each other.

He sits down at a small table, the saddest man ever. He glares straight ahead at nothing, falsely accused. Then he breaks into a large smile, as always, for the attending waitress. My father did the same. He would not say a word to me yet give voluminous reports of his cancer and his feelings on dying to barmaids. If I asked what was going on, he asked me if I was out of my mind.

Charlie, also, has an ingratiating smile for the young smiling waitress. Once I was a young smiling waitress and could make the men smile too. Their wives, like I do now, looked indulgent and impatient at the same time. I used to pity those wives. I was right to.

"I have a good heart. Don't worry," he says, "stop worrying, it will all work out."

I am so tired I think maybe he's right. Maybe I am over vigilant. Till in bed.

We come home and I use the birth control. There are things to be resolved.

He makes love to me almost gently and if I wasn't so goddamn ambivalent, I would say he was making love well. But to me he is covering too much of my mouth, affronting me by suckling my breasts, how dare he try and get intimate with me. He moves inside me and in rhythm to his going in and out, I am saying to myself I hate you I hate you. My head is hidden in his shoulders, what must he feel with a woman whose mouth never seeks his, who is always turned away. With one of his Playboy magazines or a waitress that is how he comes, with me withholding and frozen underneath.

We fall asleep, encamped.

I don't know what to do with this body of mine that so enrages me.

PART TWO

 To Any Lengths

By now you know, I am solving a crime. I have a series of clues and they are, as Einstein says, all simple once you finally understand them.

When I was twenty-five, I went to see my father. I visited him in a bar naturally and I said, "Please just tell me where your marriage papers are filed. I'll send for them, I need them to get legalized in the States."

"Well darling actually," Down on Mainstreet playing behind us, "we never were."

"Never were what? Married?"

"No."

"Why didn't you tell me? You could have saved me a lot of money with these goddamn immigration papers. I could have had the lawyers try a different way than you vouching for me as my father."

Although I never doubted he was my father. No two people could have more shifty eyes.

"I thought you got married in Amsterdam, and divorced in Montreal."

"No. We didn't want you to feel stigmatized."

Don't tell Chuck I am seeing Alan. Don't tell Mary I am

taking you on this trip. When I raise my eyebrows at you after dinner, go to the garage and get in the car. Wait there. We'll go out for a drink. Don't say anything. Tell your school that your back is badly hurt. We'll go away. Cross Canada. Cross the States. Cross your heart. Darling, I was ill. You wrote the school play? You play the piano for all the parent functions? I was away I'm sure of it. I remember now.

I am Czech. I am French. I didn't sleep with him. Honestly. I was at home. I tried to call you but no one answered. I am a rock I am an island, I wrote it. I wrote a revolutionary version of Hamlet. I went to Mcgill. Must have been a different department. You're my mother of course I do. I just slept with you, don't you think I do? Stop asking me so much. Four abortions. No, not more. I want a baby. Yes I'll marry you. I want out. Go, just go away. Leave me alone. I don't give a damn about any of you. I'm interested in this product. Can you repeat again how it works?

I didn't mean it.

It's alright.

I understand.

I don't lie anymore.

CHAPTER 12

I remember my mother's lover was visiting her in her all-glass apartment overlooking Montreal. I used to love to sit in that apartment as a child, when she was asleep or out, I would sit and watch the snow fall heavily, a faint grey of buildings behind the steady white snowfall, protected and insulated I felt by that sleeting blanket. I used to love watching the night-lights of the city try and hold their own through the ceaseless snowy downpour that would cover everything.

My mother's husband of the time was in South America. The day before she had sat close to me on the couch, smelling of sex, she always smelled of sex, I thought it was just an overpowering mustiness from her wool clothes, putrid smells emanating from an evil soul. Anyway she sat disturbingly close to me and said she had committed suicide that morning, she is so unhappy with Pierre, he does not understand how intelligent and creative she is, a type like her needs special circumstances, yes, she had taken pills that very morning.

However. She never took enough.

And then the next day my mother's lover came. I noticed she was not even sick.

Her boyfriend was 34, I was 13. We shook hands; he wore a dark green silk scarf round his neck.

She went on to make lunch, an extraordinary occurrence. I told a story, at her encouragement, about a pianist, and she kept laughing, insisting I was saying penis.

I was wearing a dress of hers, too old for me and not flattering to my voluptuous body, a geometric-designed clinging wool dress, a large circle at the throat showing my cleavage. Fulsome, ripe, about to become my mother's sexual terrorist.

My mother told me he was the best lover of all. I did not understand what constituted such a talent but no man of genius would possibly choose my mother for a lover, she of the banal stories, he must be a hack, but I swam with him in the heated indoor swimming pool on top of that glass apartment building, snow falling outside.

The two of us in the green water, my eyes hurting from the chlorine, awkward and plump I was in my mother's borrowed Givenchy bathing suit. He was smiling, crinkles round his mouth, green eyes tailored to match the swimming pool, taking my hand to help me into the water. He was naked.

Dark seaweed floating under water.

He seemed very happy that afternoon with the married Austrian woman and her haunted daughter. She was at the side of the pool, smoking a cigarette, her patent leather white shoes and St Laurent slacks peeking out at me above the pool tiles. Sunglasses indoors. Scarf around her dyed red hair.

"Jim let's go," she said.

He smiled at me. "I guess we're off to my apartment."

"It's old and a terrible mess. You'd like it," she says to me. "But you should stay here."

"No I want her to see it."

He smiles at me. We're in the water. She's up there perfect, hardened. She has an agenda. We want to submerge.

"Let her come. I like her in that dress of yours."

My eyes gleam darker. She looks annoyed. "What will she do there?"

"I can read."

"What a ridiculous idea."

My hair is shining, I know it. All afternoon at his apartment, on his overstuffed chair, he shows me copies of articles he has written, plays me jazz he likes. She hates anything but Julio Iglesias, Aznavour, cheap seduction music. Stan Getz at his most cliché. She can't tell the difference. We gossip about movies. She lives in one, but I go to them, and I make very sure, I have learned how, in my way, to make sure he never takes his eyes off me. I know to keep mine glowing, laughing, mistrusting. If you ask for nothing, it incites some men's striving. It is the way with men. I know there is only a small window for this, but now is the beginning of my time.

My mother's seduction is aggressive. Mine is to wait in the grass. It has a longer numbing affect. She talks them into sub-mission, I listen them into submission.

My mother says from the couch, "This is so boring. Darling," to me, "why don't you go to my apartment or a walk or something? We want to be alone. You understand."

"Don't push her out," he says. He is punishing my mother I realize 20 years later, but at that moment, it was my victory.

A new one. Andy was 24, I was 16. She was only 41. He was an earnest Ontarian with a flat accent. He looked like a floppy

     TO ANY LENGTHS

dog. A strange match for my Austrian mother who reminded me of a baboon with her big performer's smile and her skullcap hair. Usually she liked British humorists, Hungarian photographers, American ex-rabbis or ex-communists, French journalists, German moguls, Nigerian professors. However, Andy worked for her in films. She bought him a television, among other things. I sat in her white Peugeot and waited while she delivered it.

I was not jealous of her having a boyfriend near my own age. A father's daughter, Andy was too young for me even then. He and I went to double features, sharing popcorn, sharing celluloid fantasy. He talked like he was in the business and even then I found that suspect. Old men, young men talking as if they were in the business. I knew a real man wouldn't have time for a sixteen-year-old moving and testing her mouth in front of a mirror. He didn't really like my mother either, I knew that. He was furthering his career; he was a lady's man. Strange for a short, mop-haired guy with nice eyes and an indistinct face. But he went onto many wives, a film company of his own. He had ambition. Later, on Canadian film boards, he vetoed my mother's films down as superficial, self-aggrandizing. She took pleasure in any anecdote of his failure.

When I was 25 and long gone from Montreal, he was 33. He called me and said he was in the States, right there in my small town, he was visiting. I took him to some jazz, he told me people would buy my books because of my picture on the back jacket, he would buy one. I maybe even read him a bad short story I wrote, we drank a lot, and I went to bed with him. I still didn't like him in that way. But I wanted to know.

There wasn't much to know. A stupid thievery. She wouldn't even miss the item of value.

CHAPTER 13

Most women in prison, I am told, want to abort their babies or just leave them in the prison nursery and not come back.

Men, on the other hand, seem to laugh in prison, if not cutting each other up over stealing aftershave. Women mostly help each other out. The women put up a sign commemorating a fellow in-mate who hemorrhaged to death, taken too late to hospital for a difficult birth. Clamps on her feet, shackles on her wrists. They know after they get out, it'll be easier to get drugs than get a job. Easier to work the streets than take a typing test where the employer's eyes already said no. Easier to murder if it ever comes down to it although most women start in on themselves first. They're going to die anyway. HIV positive, most of them. Not even good enough to breast-feed their babies.

Be sure to answer the telephone even though your eyes are burning, your voice is hoarse. Wait for the mail but it's not what you hoped for although what you hope for is nameless. Marry a man you're not in love with because you're not destined for flush love. On the other hand, wait passively for flush love to surprise you at your door. Get restless when it doesn't and begin knocking on someone else's door. You're a problem to their door. Scream at your lover that he's worthless, he's abandoning you by not stepping up to the plate for you, he's not fucking giving you what you need, he's not man enough, he's a fucking child. Scream across the highway while he walks away from you. Scream in the apartment and you don't care if the neighbors hear every word. Grab the wheel of his car and swerve the car wildly to the side of the road terrifying the family motorists to just let you out of the car right now if he's going to talk that way to you. Do you understand? Disturb the peace, a peace you're never going to be part of.

CHAPTER 14

I wasn't much for criminal trespass. Never been the type to want to go where I am not wanted. I remember how it feels when you're caught. You can never escape that feeling of being the outsider.

Like when she placed bets at the Paris horse races, up and down the stairs. Up and down. Inside her. She was told to stay in bed. She wants to spontaneously abort, like she did the time before. My father won't let her. At 48, he wants a child. Finally they pull me out of her womb, cut it open to get me out. They pull me out while she's asleep.

Now that was criminal trespass.

CHAPTER 15

She loses everything, they say about me. No use in giving her anything valuable. She loses it. When I visit my mother, I mislay my identification. It's an upheaval. First sitting at lunch with her and then realizing I lost it. My money and passport are in a book, where's the book. She looks pained, how can I be so stupid. My boyfriend rolls his eyes and grimaces. I rush out of the restaurant in the middle of the meal to look for the forgotten book. I stop at the payphone to cancel my American Express. Did I leave the book at the movie theatre? My ticket must be in the book too. I ask the manager at the movies. No, no. They don't have the book. Back to the restaurant. The ladies room? Under

To Any Lengths

the table? No. Finally we go home, everyone, including myself, exhausted with me. She spent dinner telling my boyfriend how incompetent and ridiculous I am. He agrees with her. It turns out I lost the book but the passport and ticket are in the bottom of my suitcase.

She loses everything.

My father bought me a $50 watch that I wanted. He had no money but it was my birthday and I liked the watch. He spent money he didn't have. I loved that watch. Now I wear an expensive one I bought myself, but I sometimes look to my wrist hoping the one my father bought me is there, that it resisted time.

When my father was dying, I was so frightened taking care of him and no money coming in. I had left my job in the East to take care of him in the West. Who would pay for nursing care? Who would pay for the teeth that fell out, the taxis to and from hospitals? I called the antique dealers, while my father sat pale and thin in a chair, waiting for me to move him to an old age hotel, one he had chosen. He planned to die before ever needing hospitalization. That was his business plan. Don't pay for a funeral, he said, I gave my body to science. I was so undone it never occurred to me to get a marker, it never occurred to me to argue with him about a gesture of respect. I let him think he could disappear carelessly. He watched me desperately sell the chest he had brought from England, sell what was left of the silver. I sold it all for barely any money, perhaps to pay off a silly Saks bill, my rent, who knows, so thin and nervous was I. He watched them take away the carved antique chest which had been in his family for a 1000 years, the last he had of his mother, watched them take it out of his disintegrating apartment. The end of his temporal British past, nearing the end of his temporal life.

Willful destruction of property.

He never complained about my dizzying panic. He was dying and I worried about money. He moved into his hotel room with the macramé blanket a daughter of a girlfriend had knit for him. His one chair. A dusty globe.

After the antique dealer left, he lay down on his bed, exhausted. He closed his eyes. "Are you alright?" I asked.

"It's funny," he said, "my mother and father are here talking on the bed. You are too."

Oh God. I love him so I thought.

We are a family who will suffer anything.

CHAPTER 16

Still a virgin, I began making love to principles. I lived with a Greek Marxist who had pock marked skin, a soft way of speaking, and a very angry calling. Every day he gave me a new reading list. Fanon, Marcuse, Marx, Mao. He left me to attend his provocateur theatre rehearsals where the actors went about hitting planted dummies in the audience to unsettle, they said, the English complacency. Upon his return in the evening, he quizzed me about what I understood. We had no money, of course. We lived in the Montreal ghetto, revolutionaries with a huge hole in the apartment wall which some boyfriend hit instead of me. A boyfriend I agreed to drink with, not sleep with. Kill the personal.

With my newfound political awareness, I felt justified in stealing food. Skim the profits. Most of the time Vassili and I ate macaroni with butter. Ketchup as a treat. But occasionally I stole us steaks.

I stole my mother's checkbook and forged her name. Cashed it for dollars at the bank.

They contacted her. She contacted my father. What is wrong with her? She asked him.

My father contacted a man in Montreal who found me and said here is a ticket to Boston; you have to get out of this environment. A ghetto. Revolutionaries. Kill the English. Bombs in their mailboxes. Start a new life.

Vassili was eventually going to expect me to sleep with him, sex is communal. I owned only one piece of clothing. My back hurt from years of trouble.

Do you know young lady that you are committing forgery? It's a crime.

I stared blankly at the businessman. A crime? A crime is how the man hit me across the bar because I won't be his lover.

A crime is my back that hurts since a small child for reasons I don't remember.

There is only one crime I screamed at him: Society not loving its disenfranchised.

     To Any Lengths

CHAPTER 17

I got a terrible sunburn sitting in the tiny prison yard. An in-mate's mother pointed to her reddening arms. David said to her, "It's the air man it's different not as much ozone or something."

Male guards are on that day, they're easier than the women guards, they let me sit close to him.

"I'm going to marry my boyfriend," I say.

"Last month you were broken up, now you're going to marry him?"

"Well, yes. But listen nothing has to change between us. I can still visit you, we can keep writing."

"Everything will change," he says.

"Well, we're platonic now, we'll stay platonic."

"I don't want to be platonic," he says.

"Listen," I say, "we have three choices. You stop seeing or writing to me altogether; we become good friends; or a third which shall remain nameless."

"What's that?" he says.

"I'm not saying."

But I'm thinking, When he gets out, I get out.

"Listen," I say, "it's awful. I do have feelings for you. You know that. I'm close to you in a way I'm not with most men. Maybe it's the prison. You're safe. I don't think so. I think it's you. I have a funny feeling we could get along on the outside but it wouldn't happen anyway, even if I was single and you were out."

"Why not?"

"You wouldn't go for me."

"Why not?"

"Well I'm not pretty enough."

He takes my hand and says he'll squeeze it when I'm wrong.

He squeezes.

"I'm too intense."

Squeeze. "Both my wives were intense. I'm intense."

"Okay. We would get along, you're right," I say. "But somehow I don't trust it."

 To Any Lengths

"That's you," he says. "You don't trust anything. It's a survival tactic. People use it in here. You're scared to be alone. I can't offer you anything from here. There's nothing I can do. Except I would never let you be alone when I get out. That's why you're marrying him. You're frightened of being alone."

"No, that's not why. I don't know why I'm marrying him."

But I am lying. I do know. It's because he loves me, wants to give to me, it will make us both grow. Even away from each other.

"We'll probably be divorced by the time you get out."

"It's impossible to get divorced once you're in—" David says.

"You got divorced twice."

"Take it from someone who knows. It's impossible."

My head hurts. I push my body in closer to him. I want to make love with him.

"It's a mistake," he says. "You're wild, you've got balls, everywhere else you have, you come to this prison, you're working in Rikers, balls in your writing, but not here. He wants you so as not to deal with the pain of dealing with his father. He's in competition with his poet father. You understand his wound better than any other woman would. No other woman would put up with that wound. He's too wounded . . ."

"What are you saying?"

"If that wound wasn't there, you wouldn't have any interest

in each other."

My fear exactly. My head hurts even more.

"Well if it's a mistake, I'll be divorced by the time you get out."

"Don't even tell me if you get divorced. I'm not going to have anything to do with you when you get married or even after you get divorced. I'll know you're living out of fear and that will be it for me. I'm on the front lines here, I could get stabbed any night."

"Alright." My head hurts. We don't go to the vending machines to share popcorn.

Instead, to pass the time, we begin fantasizing a weekend furlough. A hotel room, lobster dinners, champagne, the ocean. I'll bring you back Monday, I say. We imagine that loft in Soho. I wonder, he says, if you could stand the sound of my working on sculpture. We imagine the day he gets out. Driving to the Jersey shore, he runs in breathlessly.

I don't say that I no longer drink champagne; I no longer drink at all. He doesn't say he won't be allowed to go to the Jersey shore. He'll have to be escorted to a halfway house for the first part of his parole.

"We could keep sharing" I say, "our artistic connection. And it'll be hard for me too when you fall for some young thing . . .but I'm prepared to experience that."

"I am too crazy about you to start seeing you married." He

     To Any Lengths

goes on to tell me about a male friend he lost when he slept with the guy's girlfriend.

All of a sudden he starts referring to his wife. He used to refer to her as his ex.

"Why are you with him?" he asks again.

"There's someone true in there," I say, "someone deeply original. I like that. I am attached to that."

It sounds airy-fairy.

We are focused and hurting like a couple breaking up. We both have headaches when we say goodbye. I put my arms around him when I say goodbye. I kiss him but not with an open mouth. We are fucked.

All the hot drive home, I want to cry.

I lie down exhausted on my bed.

I return my intended's call. I tell him where I was, what David said.

"What a misogynist," my boyfriend says. "What a con. He takes part of what he knows you feel and manipulates it to make it sound like you are making a mistake. He's a great con, one of the greatest. Listen," he says, "these wild minds you love are selfish. You drive out there and then he just turns on you. He's in prison. Who does he think he is? That's where what he knows got him. The selfish bastard. Are you hurt?"

"Yes."

I am surprised. My boyfriend is being kind to me. When did this happen?

"Well, now you know. Now you know who he really is."

"Why is it every time I see him I dream you are my brother?" I ask petulantly.

"That's because," my boyfriend says, "I can't take you to the sexual heights these men can. These golden talkers you love. They're your father. You love being with the wild men. You think they understand you. They connect with that old part of you that sat up at the bar with your father."

"What am I doing with you then?"

"I have a golden heart," he replies.

We agree to meet for dinner.

The phone rings again. It's David. "Hey I'm sorry man. I shouldn't be laying this trip on you about marriage. You won't visit me again."

"No, I will. I will. Let's take a few days to think this over. Think over what happened."

My head hurts. On the drive home from prison I listened to a woman on a talk show speak about rape. What do I know about rape?

All I know is I couldn't have David. He's in prison and I'm in a relationship. I want David because he doesn't live in a corner of the room. He's high tailing it. I want to high tail it. But I don't trust David. Lying is easy for him. I don't want to lie anymore. He is a part of me in his wanting to go big time. Failing big time. In wanting the high time. I marry my boyfriend because I know there is no David in reality for me. High tailing it to prison. I must not encourage that part of myself. I am closing something down, to maybe open something else up. The David I want and maybe could have but whom I turn away from. I am raped.

By myself, I think.

CHAPTER 18

I used to wear sheer see-through blouses into the old Luchow's. A neat skirt and delicate flesh toned gauze tops. You could see, as they say, everything.

I sat in the Copley Square courtyard in jeans and a white see-through Indian shirt with nothing underneath. I made friends easily then. Everyone was interesting. A very attractive man who lived in the Eliot hotel said he used to be a bandito. He had a huge scar across his chest. He showed it to me although I never was his mistress. I was interested in the details of his life. Broad and dark he was, I learned nothing except that scar.

Why the see-through blouses? Sheer dresses with nothing

underneath. I wore them to middle class weddings in Kiwanis and Elks clubs. Staunch Irish and misplaced Scots watched the girl with no clothes on dancing. What I wore out, these people would never wear in their bedrooms.

This desire for nakedness. I haven't worn panties since a child.

People think indecent exposure is to entice. But I know it is to keep things off you.

If you haven't had a mother, you end up soiling what's on you.

CHAPTER 19

I would be sitting at a beige desk in a beige office or just waking up and I knew. I would eat toast to try and stabilize the queasy feeling. Even before taking a pregnancy test, I would book the abortion.

I had no moral feelings on the subject. Pregnancy was a side effect of sex. Why would I risk breaking those moments when I had taken some man's breath away, when he was totally rapt with me, why would I all of a sudden become prosaic enough to interrupt this given tenderness to get up and put a diaphragm in? Why would I risk losing even three minutes of attention? I took hairy arms and penises and deep voices wherever possible.

In cars. In movies. In towers. In gardens. On beaches. In boats. Anywhere. I could manage the consequences. Why would I risk 20 minutes of affection, why risk 20 minutes where I was desired, valuable, just because I might have to suffer two weeks of physical ungainliness? Even when poor, I could always find $200. I did many times. Many times.

I didn't always tell anyone. I was ashamed it happened so often. One friend knew and said that singlehandedly I could populate an entire country. It did seem strange how fertile I was, especially when so against completion of the project. I hardly told any of the men, many of them one-night stands, and never anyone I would want to build a life with.

Love was never involved.

I'd go to different clinics so as not to draw attention to myself. I'd lie to the in-take nurse about how many I'd had. Give an amount that would get me a kind reprimand and a patient discussion of changing my birth control and then I would grit my teeth as the doctor began his work. I would hold tight to some strange nurse's arm. Be amazed at her kindness.

I would rest, get up before the other women, and on sea legs, take myself out to lunch. It wasn't the food. It was sitting down totally alone. Marking the ritual that I was starting all over again. It was my life now to do with.

At lunch, I would feel slowed down physically, humbled. I would be strangely vulnerable.

I loved that quiet, insulated feeling after an abortion. It would be the one time I would make time for myself, share an intimacy with myself. Sometimes I would have plans that night, give a dinner party, feel a cramping in my legs at the end of the evening. But sometimes, I would just go to bed with a book. Listen to the cove lap. Be very, very quiet. Tomorrow would be a different day.

"There is some correlation with all of that," I say to my intended, "and my not wanting a baby."

"I don't see it," he says.

I hardly do myself. He doesn't see it because he only sees wanting a baby.

"Well I could have been trying to do to myself what my mother wanted to do to me. I could have been being faithful to my father, having babies with men in the dark and then aborting them because it is not the right thing to do, being faithful to my father by loving the wrong men who feel like the right men . . .anything . . . Anything, I don't know."

I look at him terrified at the lengths I will go to.

 To Any Lengths

CHAPTER 20

I am getting married, it's true. There are phone calls. This one tells me of the new sundress she's going to wear, another calls to make sure I put the first wife in a separate part of the restaurant. There are phone calls about the night before the wedding. My boyfriend wants to give a party and I can't imagine anyone wanting to come.

I am doing the hardest thing, blending my life with another, consciously, without the aphrodisiac of desire and lust. Doing it because it is the responsible, next step thing to do.

A man I know doesn't want to give up drugs. I quietly say to him, "Well if I'm getting married for some new feelings, you could certainly try giving up codeine."

Let's all take one step forward.

I am almost one with myself about this wedding. I walk down the street and the hordes of men, the men wearing huge sunglasses who pass you clutching their bicycles, or the men walking just walking anywhere, those men who always comment, "Looking good," "Your husband sure is lucky," "Mmm mmm mmm," now they say, "You sure look happy."

It does feel like progress.

Then the phone rings.

David.

"Are you mad at me?" I ask.

"Why should I be?" he says. "Did you get my card? The feeling in it reminds me of us."

"Not yet."

"I keep thinking about dancing with you," he says.

Dancing, I think. I never dance with my boyfriend.

I go back to David's light voice.

"Then," he says, "I wrote you a long letter, 6 pages, a real crazy one. I just sat in front of the typewriter and it flew."

"Good, I love those. I miss you."

"Okay baby," he says, "I miss you too."

Here on the end of a telephone from prison is a man I can

dance with.

"When are they coming?" I ask.

"The tenth." I mean his daughter and ex-wife or wife depending how mad he is at me.

Lots of people have loved married women, I tell myself. Novels have been written about it. He put himself in prison. I didn't do it. If he had wanted to wait for me, steal a woman like myself from a man like Charlie, he should have thought of that before he made millions of dollars and had a high time manufacturing marijuana. He should have stayed free and met me and wooed me with true, focused attention.

"I can't talk too long," he says, "I'm running out of money—"

"I'll send you some. I'll try to get to a post office."

"If you can."

"So what are you doing to me," I say. "I walk down the street and I get these powerful thoughts of you. I write your name on a blank piece of paper while I wait for packages at the post office. Why did you do this to me?"

"You haven't seen anything yet," he says.

And I like him for that. This is a man who will take the man part in the play. It doesn't matter to me that the play may close, that he may never have to deliver on the promise. This is a man who knows you have to dance love in, twirl it gracefully and aggressively past the guards, to have it melt, sun, weave, bind your soul.

"Well okay," I say, "I'll come see you soon."

"Good, baby."

"Okay, so let's talk later," I say.

"Okay."

No lingering this time on the 10-minute phone call. We get off quickly. Me, for not telling him the truth that I am enjoying getting married. He, because he doesn't want to hear it.

I put the black phone on the black receiver. That call broke into my wedding plans. It danced into my wedding plans like an assault.

CHAPTER 21

The mail comes and in it David has sent a cartoon about why the dinosaurs perished. It seems their manuscripts were continually rejected.

He sends an article about children learning Greek mythology. One of the children is asked (she is Aphrodite) why she cheats on her husband Hephaestus (my boyfriend) with the god of War, Ares (David). "Why did you get married if you can't be faithful?" A seven-year-old god from the audience asked.

"I felt sorry for him," Aphrodite said. "He's just so little."

My boyfriend tries to make me laugh too. He reads me a clipping from the paper about a moose who fell in love with a homemade deer placed in someone's garden to frighten away birds. The moose wooed this deer, sniffed her, studied her, finally began ramming her, till the front of the deer statue fell to the ground.

The moose stopped, looked around and trotted away forever.

Two things drove me to this story.

One was of course what to do with the sexual energy of knowing David. How to contain it. The other was an image on Second Avenue. The image inside the mind of a pederast.

What you will get instead is a book about my mother.

Anyway what I saw was a person being soothed, encouraged, mesmerized by a creamy child, whose softness, trust is exquisite. I saw her being almost blinded by a child's unbounded perfect energy.

I kept seeing that person made darker, made diseased, distorted by that child's innocence. Made hollow and cruel by that shining child soul looking directly up for love. Someone who knew her own death inside.

I can understand falling in love with a child. Big smiling eyes ready to love you, eyes willing to love you, eyes that want to love you, and here this pederast woman cannot. Just can't. Passionate eyes, eyes laughing to live, or crying to love, must be cruel when everything is dead inside. I can understand wanting to punish.

I can understand using sex.

After all, babies are optimistic. Good or bad, share my skin, my responsiveness with me. But I can understand the snake, unasked and furious rising, okay I'll share but watch how I'm going to make it hurt. You will never be the same. You will see. What all people must suffer.

I kept seeing that child, golden and exquisite, and someone wanting to touch her. To take in that sunny purity just one last time. In case it healed. But it doesn't, so instead ruin that child, revenge what was murdered, show that child what has been ravaged unheard negated taken. Come near her twisting and gangling freshness. Rub her hairless delicate vagina as invasion a reprimand of all the dead children and dead mothers and dead who deserve to be dead pleasure for the child. Away from childish things. Fear. The end.

I saw the person doing it. Not clearly. No name. I felt a strange compassion for this train wreck of a soul. A person so wounded and defiled herself, so torn from her natural beauty that she must covet, drain, siphon off a child's.

"Well," a barmaid once said to me when I was a child sitting at the bar waiting for my father to show up, "looks like your mother sure knew how to take away your childhood."

I nodded my assent.

Some questions are never answered. Some atrocities never explained. David once told me he had to kill a man hand-to-hand in a Vietnam tunnel. He never looked at the face of his so-called enemy.

There is an eye for an eye. An abortion for rejection. Murder for murder. Jail for murder. Pederasty for a clamped soul.

CHAPTER 22

Can you lend me $200? I'm pregnant. Of course it's yours. Can you lend me $300 to fix my car? I will pay you back. I'm sorry I ran your car into the fence. I was looking for something in the back seat and I hit a tree. I'll pay for the repairs as soon as I can. I'm sorry it's over, after all you have done for me.

If we marry, I will travel more. I will feel it nothing less than a ferocious obligation to do whatever I please. Did you hear me? I will NOT make you dinner I will NOT take your name I will NOT tolerate how you are rude to taxi drivers whose language you can't understand. I will tell you when you appall me. I will even fall in love with someone else if I have to. You will not HAVE me. You think my freedom used to bother you, well now, now that it is at risk, I will do nothing less than extort it from you.

 To Any Lengths

CHAPTER 23

David writes:

17 Questions

1. Now that you have been in prison for a while . . . What do you do in your spare time . . . ?

MANAGE MY PORTFOLIO . . . PRETEND I'M CLINT EASTWOOD AND POSE IN FRONT OF THE MIRROR SAYING THINGS LIKE "A MAN'S GOT TO KNOW HIS LIMITATIONS" UNDER MY BREATH . . . LOOK FOR MAGAZINES WITH THOSE SAMPLE

SMELL PERFUMES IN THEM THAT HAVEN'T BEEN USED UP . . . WHAT THE HELL DO YOU THINK I DO . . . I RUN THE PRISON GRIFT . . . TO STAY ALIVE . . . TO GET PROTEIN . . . TO GET FOOD . . . TO STAY ALIVE IN THIS HELL'S KITCHEN ARENA . . .

2. How did you spend last year's New Year?

IN THE SPANISH TV ROOM . . . IT MADE MORE SENSE TO BRING IN THE NEW YEAR NOT BEING ABLE TO UNDERSTAND ANYONE'S RESOLUTIONS . . . ACTUALLY . . . I ENJOY THE SPANISH PEOPLE A LOT . . . THEY'RE ALIVE . . . DON'T COMPLAIN . . . AND ARE VERY PASSIONATE . . . A CUBAN GUY CUTS MY HAIR . . . HE WAS IN THE ARMY AGAINST BATISTA . . . WE EXCHANGE WAR STORIES . . .

3. What is it you fear most . . . Being in prison . . .

PROBABLY THE SAME THINGS YOU DO . . . CHOLESTEROL IS BIG ON MY LIST . . . YOU KNOW . . . THOSE HUNKS OF ASTEROID STUFF THAT FLOAT THROUGH YOUR VEINS WITH THE FACE OF NORMAN

SCHWARZKOPF IMPRINTED ON THEM . . . AND OH YEA PLAQUE BOTHERS THE SHIT OUT OF ME . . . THAT UNCLASSED STUFF THAT'S EVERYWHERE IN YOUR BODY . . . I THINK IT WAS LEFT OVER FROM THE BIG BANG . . .

4. How do you want to see yourself when you get old?

PEOPLE WEAR THEIR LIVES IN THEIR FACES . . . LOOK AT PICASSO . . . HEMINGWAY . . . IT HAS SOMETHING TO DO WITH APPETITE . . . WITH BEING ALIVE . . . I WANT TO BE HUNGRY AND ALIVE . . . LOOKING . . .

5. What do you think of the notion of men losing touch with themselves . . . Finding their masculinity?

DO YOU MEAN DO I THINK THAT THE MEN OF TODAY NEED BONDING OR SOMETHING . . . ALL THAT ROBERT BLY STUFF . . . SWEAT LODG-ES . . . WHERE A BUNCH OF GUYS GO INTO THE WOODS . . . BEAT DRUMS AND DANCE AND HUG . . . YEA . . . I CAN SEE ME NOW . . . DANCING AND

HUGGING WITH SOME HAIRY GUY WITH A BEARD
. . . TELL THEM TO COME IN HERE IF THEY WANT
TO FIND THEMSELVES . . . THEY'LL FIND OUT WHO
THEY ARE IN A NEW YORK MINUTE . . .

*6. Are you saying that prison is good . . . Necessary for a man
to find himself?*

NO, THAT'S NOT WHAT I AM SAYING . . . WHAT I'M
SAYING IS THAT REAL LIFE EXPERIENCE IS HARD TO
FIND IF YOU DON'T LOOK FOR IT . . . SEEK IT OUT
. . . WE LIVE IN POP CULTURE . . . AND EVERYONE
INSULATES THEMSELVES FROM ANYTHING THAT
IS A BIT UNCOMFORTABLE . . . IN HERE . . . YOU'VE
GOT TO FORGE YOUR OWN CIRCLE . . . THEN YOU
PRESENT THE MAN YOU HAVE MADE OF YOURSELF
. . . AND YOU EARN THE RESPECT ACCORDED YOU
. . . YOU'RE TESTED CONTINUOUSLY IN HERE . . .
YOU'VE GOT TO BE RESILIENT . . .

7. What's your worst nightmare?

BEING TIED UP AND FORCED TO WATCH SPIEL-

BERG'S JURASSIC PARK . . .

8. You seem to be a man who thinks life experience is important?

HOW ELSE ARE YOU GOING TO LEARN . . . LET ME TELL YOU A STORY . . . I HAVE A FRIEND HERE IN JAIL . . . HE'S BEEN IN JAIL FOR YEARS . . . HE'S OLDER NOW . . . BUT WHEN HE FIRST CAME TO PRISON . . . WHEN HE WAS 19 . . . IN CALIFORNIA . . . FOLSOM PRISON . . . HE WAS JUST A KID . . . ANYWAY . . . FIRST NIGHT IN PRISON . . . SCARED TO DEATH . . . THEY PUT HIM ON A HEAVY DUTY TIER . . . WHERE THERE ARE A LOT OF HEAVY TIME PEO-PLE . . . THIS GUY STARTS CALLING TO HIM ALL NIGHT LONG . . . SAYING HE'S "HIS" NOW AND HE'S GOING TO FUCK HIM . . . THAT HE BETTER LET HIM OR HE'S GOING TO CUT HIS THROAT . . . ALL NIGHT LONG FOR A WEEK . . . THIS GUY IS SAYING TO THIS KID . . . "SAY GOODNIGHT DADDY . . . SAY GOODNIGHT DADDY . . . I'M YOUR DADDY NOW . . . SO SAY GOODNIGHT DADDY" . . . WELL FINALLY THE DAY ARRIVES WHERE THEY'RE PUT ON THE REC YARD TOGETHER . . . THE KID RUNS UP TO THIS GUY AND JAMS A SHARPENED TOOTHBRUSH

INTO BOTH THIS GUY'S EYES . . .TO THIS DAY THE KID . . . NOW AN OLD MAN, WON'T LET HIS KIDS CALL HIM DADDY . . . THEY CALL HIM PAPA . . . IT'S NO FUCKING JOKE IN HERE MAN . . .

9. What's your most impending question right now . . .?

WHAT IT WOULD BE LIKE TO MAKE LOVE TO A VEGETARIAN GREENPEACE VOLUNTEER . . . THAT HAS BEEN FORCE FED STEAK FOR TWO WEEKS . . .

10. What's your second most impending question?

ARE THE JAYCEES REALLY SYMBIONESE LIBERATION ARMY IN DISGUISE . . . AND WHY DO THEY HAVE TO ALWAYS NAIL UP THOSE FUCKING TABLETS TO COMMEMORATE THEIR PRESENCE EVERYWHERE . . .

11. Let's change direction for a while . . . What's your favorite story of all time . . .?

THAT'S EASY . . . RIKI TIKI TAVI . . . BY RUDYARD KIPLING . . . IT'S GOT EVERYTHING . . . BRAVADO

. . . COWARDICE . . . HOPE . . . PASSION . . . MORALITY . . . NAIVETE . . . IT'S GOT IT ALL . . . YEA . . . THAT'S IT FOR SURE . . .

12. How do you communicate with people on the outside and whom . . .?

WELL . . . EVERYTHING IS CENSORED . . . BUT LETTERS . . . MOSTLY . . . AND THERE'S ONLY ONE PERSON I'M COMMUNICATING WITH RIGHT NOW . . . A WOMAN . . .

13. What's she like?

WELL . . . WHERE DO I START . . . SHE'S SO DAMN BEAUTIFUL THAT WHEN SHE VISITS . . . I GET SORT OF TRANSFIXED . . . CAN'T TAKE MY EYES OFF HER . . . ON THE LAST VISIT I WAS GETTING OFF JUST WATCHING HER BUY ME A PEPSI OUT OF THE MACHINE . . . SHE'S VERY GRACEFUL AND FEMININE . . . I MUST SAY THAT AT FIRST I DIDN'T TRUST HER . . . BUT SHE'S SLOWLY SHOWING HERSELF TO ME . . . AND THE MORE I SEE . . . THE MORE ENCHANTED I BECOME . . . BUT I

THINK SHE'S STILL AFRAID OF ME . . . I AM PRETTY CRAZY . . . AS YOU CAN TELL . . .

14. Are you tough on women?

YEA . . . FOR SURE . . . BUT THEN PASSION AND PAIN ARE CLOSE NEIGHBOURS . . . ON THE LAST VISIT HERE I BEAT HER UP PRETTY BAD . . . THINGS GOT A LITTLE OUT OF HAND . . . BUT THAT'S WHAT HAPPENS WHEN YOU'RE PASSIONATE ABOUT SOMEONE OR SOMETHING . . . A FRIEND OF HERS . . . ONCE SAID THAT I KNOW JUST WHAT TO SAY TO A WOMAN . . . AS IF I'VE GOT SOME PROGRAMMED STRATEGEM . . . HELL MAN . . . I JUST DO WHAT I FEEL . . . I'M A BLOCKHEAD WHEN IT COMES TO THIS STUFF . . .

15. Why did you beat her up if you care so much about her?

I THINK IT'S A DEFENCE MECHANISM . . . FOR ME . . . SURVIVAL TECHNIQUE LEFT OVER FROM NAM OR SOMETHING . . . I'M BEGINNING TO SHOW HER THINGS ABOUT MYSELF I HAVEN'T SHOWN ANYONE IN A VERY LONG TIME . . . MAYBE NEVER . . . IT'S

SCARY FOR ME TO TRUST SOMEONE SO MUCH . . .
AND IT'S A NATURAL IMPULSE FOR ME TO DRIVE
ANYONE OFF BEFORE THEY SEE ME TOO CLEARLY . . .

16. What do you think or hope will happen . . .?

WELL . . . RIGHT NOW SHE'S WORKING THROUGH
SOME OF HER OWN SHIT . . . IT'S SOMETHING SHE
HAS TO DECIDE FOR HERSELF . . . SHE'S TOUGH AND
SMART AS A WHIP . . . I HOPE SHE KICKS ME IN THE
BUTT IF I GET TOO TOUGH WITH HER . . . SHE KNOWS
THAT IF YOU WANT THE HEAT . . . YOU'VE GOT TO
SWEAT . . . WHEN I GET OUT OF HERE I HOPE SHE
AND I WILL TAKE OFF ON A JET POWERED LOBSTER
. . . WAVING A SCIMITAR OR SOMETHING . . . AND
JOIN THE FOREIGN LEGION . . .

17. What do you think she thinks of you . . .?

OH I DON'T KNOW . . . LIKE I SAID . . . SHE'S
GOING THROUGH SOMETHING RIGHT NOW . . .
SHE PROBABLY LIKES ME WELL ENOUGH I GUESS . . .
ALL THIS STUFF VISITING SOMEONE IN PRISON IS

EXCITING FOR AWHILE, BUT IT WEARS OFF . . . SHE DOES SAY THAT SHE THINKS I'M COURAGEOUS . . . BUT I'M NOT NEARLY AS COURAGEOUS AS MY LIFE WOULD SUGGEST . . . NOBODY IS . . . BUT . . . I MUST SAY THAT I'VE FACED MY DEMONS WITH HONESTY . . . I HOPE SHE AND I CAN FACE DOWN A BUNCH OF THE LITTLE BASTARDS TOGETHER . . . SOMEDAY. . . YEA . . . THAT WOULD BE REALLY NICE . . . SAY DID I TELL YOU ABOUT THE REALLY SEXY RED DRESS SHE WORE . . . AND SHE HAD AN ANKLE BRACELET ON . . . JUST AFTER I TOLD HER HOW MUCH I –

Cut . . . Out of time . . . Cut . . . That's a rap . . .

WAIT A FUCKING MINUTE, I WASN'T FINISHED . . . YOU GUYS ARE ALL THE SAME . . . HEY . . . DON'T SHUT THE MIKE OFF . . . HEY . . . WHAT DO YOU THINK YOU'RE DOING . . . HEY . . .

On the drive to my boyfriend's I read him David's 6-page letter and edit out the romantic parts, especially about the ankle bracelet. I show him the postcard with Frieda nestled into the crook of Diego's large person, the two artists looking out into

 To Any Lengths

the distance. My boyfriend says, "All men who fall in love with you think they share a vision with you. It's because you listen without judgment," he says.

"David has an interesting mind," he continues, "but there is something off, keep that in mind."

We discuss how David is respected by the guards and the other prisoners. How he wages war on the guards, flooding his cell, jumping the attack crews who come to get him. Playing hero to the prisoners who need a hero to fight against the sliding locks of humiliation. He will fight back. Like when he was the only one left alive in his platoon. We discuss how even the guards respect David; most of them were marines originally themselves.

Then my boyfriend shudders.

"What's the matter?"

He looks down at the speedometer. "I'm going too fast."

I look over at his unsteady jaw and wonder if this conversation is upsetting him. But he is as raring to talk about it as I am; in fact, it is one of the few things we ever pass an animated hour over together. He too must need a blast of freedom while he sits safely in his car. Much better someone else pays.

"The thing about David," I continue, "the thing I have figured out is that he likes fighting. He always mentions Vietnam. Most people who were smoking dope, sleeping with longhaired girls wearing long earrings and long dresses weren't joining up in the 60s, they were running away. He joined. He likes prison, not in its loss of freedom but in its front line confrontation."

My boyfriend listens. He likes to fight too. He often lies in bed imagining what he would do if an intruder came into the apartment. He imagines the fight. And here, here David is having them.

David is being punished.

I tell my boyfriend that ultimately this preoccupation of David's with war and women is not interesting.

"Does his wife know you visit him?" my boyfriend asks.

"I don't think so. I never asked him."

"I'll bet she doesn't. Which gives you the role of the mistress. I hope you understand that."

I squirm a bit.

"Another thing," my boyfriend says, "is I don't want him visiting us when he gets out. He's crazy. He'll destroy us for no other reason than he wants to at the time."

"Oh he won't do that," I say.

"Of course, he'll do that and you better be on your toes."

"Don't worry. I didn't fall for him when I knew him years ago. Why would I now? He probably won't even want me."

"He's going to want everything."

     To Any Lengths

Then I tell my boyfriend how my best friend tells me she could never tolerate someone who was involved with drug smuggling or drug manufacturing with what it does to kids. And how David and I have never even mentioned that aspect of his career.

"No you never," my boyfriend says, "talk about anything didactic with him. That's why he likes you. You both talk in spaces. Rev method."

"It's creative to talk like that," I say. "Anyway, you never find anything out by being direct. Especially from a type like him. People have to reveal themselves, not be cross examined."

My boyfriend accedes that that might be a good way with someone like David; a man, my boyfriend says, who only tells you 30% of what is going on.

"Is it you're worried I am studying how to be a criminal?"

"No. Keep in mind making a life out of bucking authority is a small life finally."

I nod agreement and puff on my cigarette.

"Anyway, it's better you talk out loud about this preoccupation with David rather than hide it," he says.

True.

I know my boyfriend worries that when David gets out, our life will turn into Cape Fear. I don't.

"What are you going to do," he says, "when David gets out

and says he has $300,000, let's go to Paris for a few days."

"I'll go."

"Oh you're a case," he says.

"I'll ask him if you can come along."

My boyfriend turns seriously to me, "I would love it if you ever did something like that but you never would."

We get along talking about David, in our encapsulated car discussing a passion of mine and a vicarious passion of his. Will she or will she not leave? He needs me to keep talking.

We tire of our drive and get an ugly little motel room. My boyfriend wants to make love. We are getting married in two weeks exactly. As he rolls on top of me, his kisses, his touch nauseate me. I don't even pretend to respond. I turn my back away from him while he has his way, my mind making calls to cancel the wedding.

I tell him in the morning as we continue our drive that this is it. There is something wrong with me. I am not sexual enough with him; we should not go through with the wedding. There is something wrong with me.

"There's nothing wrong with you. You're just frightened of getting close."

"But why do you want to be with me? I'm terrible, can't you see it?"

"You're not deep down. Anyway you'll change."

"What if I don't?"

"You will change. You'll become more secure."

"What about sex?"

"It will come back. Don't cancel the wedding," he says. "We will work all this out."

"I don't understand why you want me," I say.

"You're fun."

"What do you mean by that?"

"I'm teaching you something. How to be normal."

He's teaching me? Normalcy? It's not his strong suit either.

I take his hand. He does not abandon me. I must say that.

I don't cancel the wedding. It's a paltry sum I am taking from him. It is worse than prostitution. Giving myself away for the tender of love. Turning my back, closing my eyes, buying flashy clothes as recompense. A wedding dress no matter how you cut it is flashy. All this so as to get love. This is how low I sink, sleeping with a man, whom I am continually leaving, only to get paid with the currency of love.

CHAPTER 24

My mother is the last call I make about the wedding. When she finally returns the call, she tells me she was away, visiting a friend in Ottawa. It wasn't that pleasant, the friend is not a very good hostess, and the weather was so very hot. Hotter than New York.

"Yes," I say, "a friend told me that it was very hot up north."

"Must be a weather pattern," she says.

"Listen, I am going to marry Charlie. In a couple of weeks. I have to do something. Go forward in some way. We're not making a big deal of it."

"Oh."

"I'd like you to come, but if you don't want to I understand.

It's just a Justice of the Peace thing and a lunch but if you don't want to, I perfectly understand. It's such short notice. I took so long to make up my mind."

I wait a beat.

"I understand," she says gently. "I don't really want to. It's so tiring you know. Your friends will all be there."

"We'll come to Montreal in the Fall," I say ingratiatingly, "we'll do our own celebration."

"Yes that's a much better idea."

"Of course we can take that cruise you want," I say, "in the winter together. Now that I'm married I'll want to get away a lot."

She laughs.

"Well," she says, "I see what you're doing. You're marrying to leave him. I had a thought the other day that you would do that. Plenty of people I know are together for years and then they divorce once they marry. Divorce as friends. Potterton. Howard in England. They marry and then get divorced. It will finalize this endless relationship of yours. I'm not judging it, you and I are very different but you just can't leave anyone. You're not good at leaving like I am," she says. "You'll finally resolve this. You don't want a baby you would have had one by now. How many years do you have left?"

"About two or three. He has to make money if I am to

have a baby. That's our agreement. His making money makes the probability of a baby even less. He can have a baby with his second wife."

"Anyway, I won't come," she says, "it's not like you're some virgin in white having a big wedding."

"No."

Just then the buzzer rings and it is my intended. I motion I am talking to her. He sits down.

"Charlie is here. Why don't you say something to him?"

She congratulates him on being so persevering. She tells him she can't come but so many friends will be there.

I see his face get smaller. He is not used to being pushed aside. He expects to be celebrated.

I tell her I will call her when I am on the road. I am leaving the next morning on business.

She and I discuss how much we like being alone in hotel rooms on the road. How her mother said she used to stare at the wall, but I know, don't I, there was lots going on in her mind.

I know, I said.

I hang up.

"Are you insulted?" I ask him.

"A little."

"Well, I expected it. And I gave her such little notice. I knew she wouldn't want to come."

"She's so strange," he says.

"True."

But what I don't say is that I am feeling a kind of love for her. She speaks out my unconscious, that all this is a futile detour from isolation. I just don't know if it is the devil's voice she speaks or the voice of reason.

This morning on the way to the airport he was rude to the Asian cab driver who was trying to express his rationale for taking FDR instead of the tunnel. My intended could not understand what the cabdriver was saying, although I could because I was listening. I got angry with him for insulting the driver.

And only that morning I had sat across from him and tried not to feel disappointed at his thin pigeon toed bent over presence, his hand going up and down around his mouth. He had a toothache.

"Did it hurt all night?" I ask.

"Yes."

"Maybe you should call the dentist," I say.

"Not yet," he says. "It may be inflamed from not having brushed them for so long."

I shouldn't, but I do, "We're supposed to twice a day. I mean one should at least once . . ."

"I know."

Last night when we made love, I didn't turn away like the time before, but I wouldn't let him touch me. I made him stay straight backed, arched, inside me. I held his arms away from me till he came.

There is no crime today I tell you of. At least there is no name for it. Except maybe for blind mother love.

PART THREE

My fiancé has bought rings.

"I got a fine one for you," he says.

Tells me about the touchtone phone he will bring up to the wedding so I can call into my office.

This is how he shows love.

My mother, ever encouraging, said she would come to my divorce. She is giving us for a wedding gift what she has already given me a couple of months ago—the extra single bed on a free cruise she is going on.

"You'll want to get away now that you'll be married. You can't leave anyone," she says. "I'm not like that," she boasts, "I know how to."

CHAPTER 25

So. Friends are driving long distances, buying gift certificates, dresses and smoking cigarettes in alarm. His family is lending him money and taking planes.

But something is missing.

What it will be is that when I stand there in my white dress, among friends who are kind enough to be encouraging, friends who have lived a lifetime with me, some in just long telephone calls, a knife will go in, I will feel a sharp pierce. Wasn't I supposed to die by now, don't I know what she knows, love is in the movies; sex is motivation for any killing.

You are so unique, she said, in marrying, why not just divorce.

Have you no courage?

Oh it's cold, cold, cold glass that you pushed into my rib cage in my white dress. I am not bleeding red on the white dress; nothing shows, that is my way. I don't turn her in; she trusts that, she knows I am curious always curious to see what lengths she will get up to next. I turn to her specter, grab my rib and cut my hand as I pick it out like it is nothing, the glass, oh don't bother, it's nothing, an accident. I look to her. My life is only an accident. She smiles, anyone's is, how foolish of you to want to play predictably. Revolution she sneers, bourgeois revolution, are you hurting yet? Sleep with married men in the room not your boring husband you fool. I begin listening, some glass still in my rib cage, sinking in, now through my blood vessels, but my heart is safe, that is shielded from her, shielded off from her glass, but I find myself leaning toward her while my husband laughs and jokes with the guests. I watch her watching me watch her shine her lips in her compact glass mirror. Her eyes shine too. She has me. I am the mirror of darkness, not the heart. What a thing, my husband still talking and there is no need for words while watching her. I am already on the boat with her, watching my own wedding through the prism of her white patent leather shoes, on the boat to see where is this place she is taking me to, that is so free, so artificially sustained, that it can live so well without love.

PART FOUR

My boyfriend is allergic to cats and doesn't want the work of a dog. I mean husband.

"Mrs. Olson?" What the hell is this some joker and then I recognize, it's David on the phone.

"I didn't change my name, I told you."

"Well how was the wedding," he asks.

"A wedding. Kind of fun. You should have come. Come over now and I'll show you the pictures."

"We have to have a sit down," he says. "That's what the mafia calls it. A sit down."

"I'm not driving all the way out there to have my feet put in concrete."

"Baby, they're already in it."

"Hah. I enjoyed the party. People read poems about what an impossible couple we are and how they didn't think we'd really do it and then congratulated us for going ahead. It was sunny and lots of laughter and—You want to hear one?"

"Yes," he says.

So I begin reading tributes to our wedding where I am made out to be a playgirl and how my boyfriend stays steadfast and never gives up, a regular Kipling character in how he persevered and what was it we shared someone asked and how I eat his food and not my own, how I slip out of a noose quickly when no one is looking, a word to the wise they said to my husband but I notice David doesn't laugh where the punch lines are, is he listening and then I think What am I doing?

"Let me get my calendar," I say, "and see when I can come out."

"Why?" he says, "you never stick to it."

"It's a start. Hey," I say, "looking at the calendar, I'll come on my father's birthday."

"What day is that?"

"A Friday."

"I love Fridays. What are you wearing right now?" he asks.

"A black dress. Spanish style. I can't wear most of my clothes to prison you have to wear a bra there."

"Bring a change of clothes," he says.

We discuss the impending law changes where first-time drug offenders may have their time shortened. He says there will be a revolution in prison if they don't change the laws. The guys are waiting daily for Janet Reno to sign the bill. I don't ask what if her law change is not retroactive. We discuss nonsense neither of us knowing what to do about my being married.

"What time did you do it?"

"10:30."

"I knew it. I told a guy in here she's doing it right now."

Fairton cuts us off, and it seems that married I am still in business.

I put the phone down and sit quietly. This is when I would call my father. It would be like a drink. I would pick up the phone and call him at his office or at one of his bars and say, Daddy, I don't have any money or I'm supposed to see her this weekend will you lie for me?

Daddy I'm married now. You always said do it for money. Well I didn't. I did it, I think, to get someone to care for me. At least, I didn't do it for a father. You were enough, thank you. I didn't change my name; I wouldn't do that to us. He married your daughter, Daddy, Jesus anyone else would have thought twice on that subject. However, I liked being married at the party, the wedding party. I liked my friends but when I drove back to New York, jazz was on the radio and my body started to move uncontrollably, rock back and forth as I did in your car as a child, rock like the Paris studies say orphans do, back and forth against the car seat, my body was taken over, Maiden Voyage Bobby Hutcherson it was, and as the beat went through my soul I moved toward David, the guy in prison, not my husband. I think that has to do with you. And what about how one has to focus on sex when one is married, although I hear that becomes the last thing you want to focus on. When you're single it's conquest and

     To Any Lengths

adventure, it's elusive and presenting but, when you're married, they say it's castor oil. I might lose my eroticism Daddy. I had it in spades for you but then I never got to have you. I always knew I would never have to spend a life with you, the daily death of eroticism. Instead, I would long for you, the tenderest of love affairs. But marriage, everyone says is day in day out contrapunt. A form of suffering. However, you forgot to tell me to suffer for what I wanted. You said, take the easy route. The easy route, Daddy, is the painful route. You misinformed me. Sometimes I thought my sexual coldness to him was that you had been a little too warm sexually to me but I think you were too drunk I'm not saying you and the guys at the bar didn't think about it propose it a lot I'm not saying the veritable smoke filled air was not humid with it but what I'm saying, now that I'm married, is I want to lie down in the sand with a man like you, a wild man, I'm capable now of lying down with a man like you, I'm grown now, I can take it, but here it is daddy I want one who won't hurt me. I mean if I lie down in the sand with him and give myself to him, allow myself to believe he won't hurt me, is it possible I can get the cut glass out of my body, it would take a man who says let's fucking enjoy it look at the sun look at that ocean here taste this fresh Italian sandwich dripping with oil and olives push your feet through the sand, yeah, down, down into the sand, are your toes covered yes well daddy now what? I would look out to the sea and realize that I'm going to die as we all do, and I'm going to have to gulp as much as I can, love my husband and every man possible love them and I guess I would just tell the truth all the time even if it creates terrible havoc, it'll be my havoc, keep reiterating it as it is so, rather like a novel, it will shape the story exactly around me and just do that without a moment's flinch. There is none to waste even all the lying in the truth and so what if they can't take it I could try, to merge, try and see what happened if I was completely myself. Oh Daddy I want to love again. This nurture love of marriage feels strange, yet it was what the shrink doctor ordered. He said go for mother love. So I got married. Listen Daddy I want you but I don't want what comes with you. Selfishness, jail. Listen Daddy I'm getting strong enough to want real love.

CHAPTER 26

My mother calls all chummy now. "I thought of offering Charlie the other ticket on the cruise I want to go on with you, as a wedding present, but I want to go myself."

"Should I ask him?"

"No. He might say yes."

For an inveterate liar, my mother is unconscionably honest. I often yearn for her life-taking honesty. It seems foreknowledge.

My shrink tells me I know nothing of marriage. I don't know it's about partnership. That you unite to achieve common goals.

I say to the shrink, "When are you going to make me successful?"

"A woman," he says, "can't become successful with a man

who is a failure. You need the love of a successful man to spur you on. You'll have to pretend you're married to me."

But I don't feel married to my shrink. I feel married to my husband with whom I did not sleep last night. I was working at my own apartment. We have not moved in together yet. I don't want to hurry things. Getting married was enough for one month. He stayed at his place and watched a semi-pornographic film on his television.

But, even in my own apartment, I know I am married. I am wearing a ring. I did it.

My mother asked me if I kept my name.

"Yes," I said.

"Like I did," she said.

But my mother's last name is her husband's.

No wonder I became a writer. Somewhere there has to live some truth. Other children of liars become lawyers. They know how to extract the truth under duress. They know how to ram it down the liar's throat. The truth is set out in books and it is only a matter of interpretation. But the truth is set down. They have left home.

Writers, as my mother does, tell the truth as it is on a given day, given page, given novel.

This is, unquestionably, one type of freedom.

In the bath this morning, I saw all my friends with their children. I saw them comforting crying boys whose dinosaurs are lost, crying girls who want the red raincoat not the green.

So what does this mean on week two of marriage?

I keep thinking of my mother.

Years and years ago when barely past being a teenager, I would laugh uncontrollably at portraits of her. Stoned on marijuana, I would visit her apartment, sit on her green velvet couch, and see the paintings as caricatures. Roaring I would be that someone had captured her. She and her lover would sit there annoyed at my being unable to complete a sentence without breaking into spasms of hiccupping laughter, hilarity every time I looked up at her very long neck, her ski slope nose, her pin button eyes, her stunned encapsulation. I would laugh that there, there she was, a caricature, they had captured the woman behind the phone and it was only this, these elongated features, it was only this, me roaring, tears streaming down my face, as she and her lover sat embarrassedly by wondering what the hell was so goddamn funny.

CHAPTER 27

"I want to go to your house," I say, "for a few days by the sea."

"Why?" he asks over the phone.

"I don't know. It will be good to spend some time there. You could come up on the weekend."

My plan is to be restored by the salt air, the blue, the blue all round me, and then I will try, once again, to give him the little I know of love.

"The sea always makes me happy," I say. "Free."

"I know."

"I'll be nicer."

He laughs. "You are nicer when you're up there. Okay. I'll

meet you there.”

Progress. An agreement.

CHAPTER 28

But my nights are stormed by blonde black v-sweater poet women who tell me in my dreams that the real life is honest, separate, away from a clamoring man.

I hoped the sea would soften, quiet me and it does almost. I am happy with the fog that won't lift off the water and so the air, even on a hot day, is thick and cool to touch. I walk through the seaside galleries and catch here and there a painting that is artful. I am happy for these people whose lives are painting, living in rickety studios, free.

At night I stare out at the harbor from his house.

My husband calls after having just returned from another

porno film. Each night he sees another one. He tells me this. Why is he telling me? He must be warning me that I am not enough. I pull out the tear and mustard gas. Over the phone. One cigarette is ready to be lit in my mouth as I pull another one out of the pack.

I yell at him that we should divorce, divorce, now, now because we are not sexually compatible. "Look at you, you go to movies, movies about decadent love, sex that leads to murder, to degradation, this is where you search for how to love. This is where you want to learn about sex."

I know it is none of my business, I am hardly making sense, but it becomes my Waterloo. "It was just like," I say, "when we were younger and you asked me what decadence was, all lascivious you were saying the word decadence, thinking you were sophisticated simply by asking about it, and I hated you, hated you because no one asks about decadence, it's not a spelling bee question, anyone who has known it, really known it, knows it is hollow, boring, repetitive.

"Sex," I rant on, "is the man who makes you laugh, who communicates, who is present to you, generous of himself. In bed, he does the same. It relaxes, enlivens you. The rest is a piece of cake and ass.

"Divorce," I say, "I want a divorce."

"You are so hostile," he says. We both are silent.

"You pushed me to marry before I was ready," I finally come up with.

"What? You want a medal for that?" he asks.

"Women aren't the way you men portray them up there on the screen—"

"What do you expect me to do go to Church?"

"Why don't you just call my mother up?" I say. "Ask her how to love. She too goes to the movies. She wanted to attend our wedding by video."

His love mentors frighten me. Professed lovers who conclude their love in 2 hours, The End—

He is screaming at me, but I don't hear him I am seeing the movie of my mother's revolving door. I'm holding the phone and I see as if I am right there my father's dirty books, dirty drinking glasses, dirty looks.

"It is the loneliness that disturbs me," I say. "I thought marriage would turn you into a partner," says I, sitting by myself in his sea town.

Our voices are hoarse by the time I put the phone down. I lie back on the couch and light another cigarette. It is completely still out, the darkness is endless, it could take me to China.

I close my eyes and remember a Marilyn Monroe strapless white dress, high heels that I wore in the basement rubble of his unfinished house. Clinging hard to his body, he, holding me up by the backs of my wrapped legs. Me, holding on tight so as not to fall down on the cold damp pieces of wood. My shoes flew off, my dress smudged anyway. Did I just want to be wanted?

I see him picking me up at the airport and driving to New Hampshire for some reason, a motel, one I used to stay at with my father—he didn't know that, it was as they say a cinematic coincidence—and me so jealous there might have been the thought of another woman while I was away that I jump him in the car before we get to the room, didn't give him a chance to even say anything past the stick shift in the night and plunked hard down on top of him.

Are those the moments in the movies he is looking for? The movies we are reeling in, in spite of ourselves.

CHAPTER 29

The next day I feel kinder toward him. The angel of distortion passed. Who cares what movies he goes to?

The sun burnt my coldness out. The sea slapped me and I trusted. I biked and gulped the air.

"I figured you out," my husband says on the phone, "you can't bond."

He terrifies me with that statement and perhaps the induced terror is his power. He so terrifies me that I joke with a friend, "His next essay question is to figure out why not."

"At least he won't be bored with you," the friend said.

"No, but frustrated," I said.

"Lonely," my friend ventured.

Oh yes oh yes. I come around, but late.

CHAPTER 30

I go to my husband's place of work. I say to the guy, "I'm a friend of the carpenter's, can I just go downstairs and see him?"

"Friend?" My husband's head pops up from working on a piece of wood. "Did you say friend?"

I laugh giddily for the first time since getting married.

My father loved the locks, that's what he called the slim gates the huge ships waited in, for the water to sink down to the level of the big Canadian river. He would take us to the locks to look at the ships. I wondered if those Russian, Japanese, German sailors found me pretty. I would smile up at the huge boats.

Afterward, in front of the mirror in my new bra, listening to Aretha Franklin, I would refuse to go downstairs. Daddy, it's solitary down there.

What does sodomy mean? I remember asking my father. I did it last night and I want to know if it is wrong. Strangely, I don't remember his answer. I only remember the compulsion to tell him.

He couldn't get it up the first time with my mother, he told me.

My father was not guilty of anything untoward with me, no matter how much mining I do. This is not your average incest story. No TV movie here. I knew too much for anything I did not want to happen to happen. I even knew how to evade his thoughts. I knew which mistress he was interested in before he did. I could tell when he was falling in love before he even knew he needed to. I knew what went on or didn't go on in the bedroom with his wives by the way he poked his head in and said, "Get up!" I could sense the terrain like a reconnaissance fighter in the jungle senses exactly where the gunmen and the bombs lie, when the air is completely still or when the rains are blindingly heavy. The way a woman does with a man she loves completely. She senses all the details, all the depths and contradictions he has ever had for anyone else, all the lies he's told himself and all the lies he will tell. The way a woman knows, when she is in love, exactly what is going to happen to her.

Was it some way he had of looking at me? Or was it simply living so proximate to him for those very sexual years?

"There's nothing you can tell me," I would say to my father jokingly, "I know it all."

"When did you learn everything?"

"I came in knowing."

The prisoners in prison are right: There is no such thing as a loss of innocence story. We come in fighting.

My husband tells me his poet-father made him be quiet so he could write. He wrote in the night so he could have psychic space to explore his way out around the page. No one else could move. My husband-boyfriend-poet's son hated his father.

He is going to have to hate me.

CHAPTER 31

"David's going to change in there," my husband says. "He's going to get ground down."

"He wants to introduce me," I say, "to a serial killer. He's arranged for the guy to come out to the visiting room."

David knows I need to learn that aberrations are human.

David says the serial killer is first, a mafia guy second, and David third in the pecking order of power in the prison.

"Excellent," I congratulate him. "Although what do they do, take a vote?"

"It's the way they look at each other," my husband explains to me later. "The ones who don't project fear. Who look like they're doing well. The men just know."

I listen and realize that males are males and my husband knows what goes on in that prison better than I do.

I told David on the phone that I am so depressed about my failures at work that next time I come I will switch clothes with him and go hide in his cell. He said, "You won't last long in here."

Doesn't he think I can handle it?

"You'd get raped," he said.

Then he tells me of a man two cells over who gets hormone shots every day, has long fingernails, wears lipstick, has breasts. David's voice emotes more fear when talking about the man/woman in that cell than about his friend, the murderer.

"That guy with the hormone shots is having the best sex he ever had," my husband says.

I look at my husband and wonder what it is he knows.

My husband tells me not to worry about money. I find this strange what with bill collectors calling him to pay for his wedding vest.

"It is good you're spaced out about money," David says.

"It is?"

"Yeah. Just allow it."

I had meant to write a brilliant prison break. Dramatic and full of epiphanies but if going to prison is made up of small acts

     To Any Lengths

of crime, be they real or moral, that lead to only one that shows up clearly on the EEG, that society catches, then prison break is the same. Small acts of freedom and bravery, small acts of participating with the other and not bolting into the wall smack to your right. Small acts of change; of extending one's pacing beyond the four yards you have covered over and over for years. Telling the truth here. Showing patience there. Being naked a second longer than is comfortable. Being truthful in your body just one instant longer. Daring to wear the mantle dreamt. Being willing for the digging it takes to enlarge the prison yard.

I think David does this in prison and that was what caught me. That freedom. The freedom of anyone who smiles anyway.

PART FIVE

 To Any Lengths

"You know what he's living in there," my husband says, "is not about growth. There's no time for consciousness, finding yourself. It's about keeping up the defense."

I look at my husband and know he is talking about himself.

"Perhaps," I say.

But I don't believe him. Those who search, search everywhere.

CHAPTER 32

My mother never calls since I got married. Silence from the North.

She never called much before either. I am the one who dialed out wearily. Except when I was young and there were men for her to drone on about. She called a lot in those days and I would answer the phone and as soon as I heard, "Hello darling, are you home?" a terrible exhaustion would come over me. Then a torrent about some man, the same expostulations I had heard the week before about another man. "He is so brilliant." "He is the best lover of any of them." What did she mean and yet I knew enough not to ask. What you surround yourself with slowly becomes you. I was careful what words opinions descriptions I took from her. "He loves me so much." "Well, it ended, he wasn't very intelligent anyhow."

There is no freedom, however, for me in her silence. Last night, I fight with my husband about his wanting to help a 27-year-old model sell her furniture. I tell him he would never help a man this way. He tells me he is a friendly guy. I am convinced that this friendliness will lead him to a female perfection and responsiveness, this friendliness will awaken him to youthful, hopeful beauty and I will be left, dark, ungainly, on the side. CLOSE YOUR DESIRE FOR LIFE DOWN I want to scream like my mother.

I console myself that well, in six months, if this is to happen, all will go according to plan. Six months. If I thought this marriage was forever, I would bolt every time he induced a frightened or uncomfortable feeling in me.

I am to learn, I imagine, that I can survive these rigged juries where I am dispensed with. I am to learn perhaps my mother is wrong.

All to say that the 27-year-old is only my mother in disguise. Her sin is the sin Dante Alighieri spoke of: If you see a man in need not giving to him is equal to refusing him.

I will almost never recover from her turned face.

I can't tell you what she was looking at. I used to think a

mirror but that is what I was myself forced to turn to.

There was no conversation, no laughter to lose myself in during those forced visits with her. I looked into the mirror to reassure myself, I am substance and will not be annihilated by the volcanic razor-sharp denial of being here.

And she, the silent impenetrable mother of the perfect fingernails and tightened skin and charred heart who looked at me once and simply, decisively said "No," and then turned away only to once more when I was fully grown turn toward me again, and this was much worse, to say, "Darling don't you know I love you?"

She doesn't.

The crime is solved.

PART SIX

I had meant to write a prison break. Just push through, I said, expand yourself. There is not, according to me, any blood loss in jumping one's jail cell is there? You simply think, I'll leave this prison now; the one I've been stuck in all my life. I'll simply get up and go.

What nonsense.

As if all it takes is marrying saying yes once and then magically arriving at the outer kingdom. What was I thinking? That saying yes in front of an 80-year-old Justice of the Peace would easily entail my body, as loving one's mother does.

Everyone knows you have to prison BREAK.

I tell you this from my cellblock. I am not in his bed saying this.

I watch the French women in the film make noises as they have sex, smile smugly afterwards in their elegant dressing gowns, open their doors hungrily to strangers. I watch the man put his hand on her leg and she knows what this is; I watch all this, this huffing and puffing for pleasure in the body. I watch the women smile at the men invitingly, as if they want to be touched, loved, as if they need the men when I don't need anyone—a fool's game.

Should I use my husband to unlock this untouched body? He doesn't deserve my vulnerable body, no one does, my body has been rescinded, appropriated by the defense.

       To Any Lengths

I am going to have to find the tunnel out, the vulva in.

PART SIX

CHAPTER 33

David tells me I am important to him. He says he loves the way I hold myself. It might be my genuineness, he says, my love of art.

But everyone knows part of being a con is knowing what to say and saying it.

The courts said David needed pathological amounts of adrenalin after the war to feel alive. He needs to be endangered, he needs the impossible. Seducing a woman from behind bars.

"You sound different now you're married," my mother says on the phone.

"What do you mean?"

"You sound more well behaved."

"What do you mean?"

"I can't explain it," she says, "you're different. Maybe I am."

"Well he's very persevering," I say about my husband, as if it's his fault we got married.

"Yes he is. Do you call him your husband?"

"No. I call him by his last name."

She laughs.

"He's very persevering," she assents.

"Yes," I say, "he's the kind of guy who would go down with the Titanic on principle. I would be yelling come, get into this lifeboat and he would argue with me and go down to prove his point."

She laughs.

She doesn't realize how much I like him for that.

"You know I love you very much," she says.

I didn't tell my husband, but I went to see David a day ago.

This is the first time David and I have seen each other since the marriage. This was to be our sit down but neither of us said what we expected to say.

I got through the guards easily this time. They were even

helpful. They gave me a clear plastic bag for my change. Smiled at my confident manner at the desk. No woman was on duty. There was acceptance between the two big Black women and me waiting for the deafening electronic clang that unlocks each door. The women were dressed in their best high-heeled pumps, red dresses cut at the arms and cleavage. I had worn a simple dress that I might wear to work.

David came out on time too. I did not have to wait, as I usually do. We are both learning the system.

We sat down outside, as is our way, and said nothing for a bit. We just sat close together, confused.

He pointed to a part of the outdoor fenced-in visiting yard, and said, "Some guys were caught trying to make love with their women there, the women were bent over and the guards stopped them."

"What happened?"

"The guys were thrown in the hole and had visiting rights suspended for a year." He laughed sadly.

"I guess it's not worth trying then."

He laughed. "Why not?"

I got us lunch from the vending machines. I got popcorn and asked him to cook it in the prison microwave for me. "We'll have to hire a cook," he says, "if we live together." He had a saran

wrapped pepper steak sandwich and we sat down on the bolted
down visiting room chairs. He asked me if my husband knew
I was here and I said no. David said he didn't want to fuck up
my marriage. I said I didn't think it was in his power to. I didn't
think this was fucking it up. Didn't he like my coming to see
him? Was it fucking him up?

"No. I love it. We're doing the bit together."

I nod.

"I'm vulnerable here," he said. "I don't want anyone fucking
with me, though. You've got a normal life but I don't."

"I'm not fucking with you."

Our sit down consisted of his saying he didn't want to give
me up, but he didn't want to be bad for my marriage. We hardly
talked about my marriage. We talked about us. I said that a lot
of things are going to change in the 2-3 years David still has left
so let's leave it at that. Either we'll be friends or I'll be divorced
and we'll see.

"Anyway I don't feel like you're married," he said.

"Me neither."

I'm the one who should go to jail, so ready to throw over
the existing order.

"Are you as defended with him as you are with me?" he asks.

All of a sudden I could hear how often I tell David he won't want me, how often I bring other women into it. David always says to me, "If you want to use how you'll be too old for me when I get out, go ahead if it helps you get away."

I look at David for a second.

"It's not the same with him," I said, "I've put in a lot of years with him." But God, am I defended with Charlie he asks while here I am visiting this prisoner whose arm is on my bare leg, who is saying it's a long time since he touched soft skin. Yes, I would say I am defended with Charlie.

"He had to marry you he had chased you so long," David says.

"True."

This visit is different. Not really more well behaved, as my mother would think. But more acclimated. David doesn't talk about the other prisoners like he used to. He doesn't want to think about them. I force myself to listen to his stories about himself. How he got here.

There was the growing of marijuana of which the idea came to him when helping a friend move his plants, and then David began reading hundreds of books on agronomy and thought he'd really go to town. He liked putting the whole thing together, like a mission, he said. He thinks drugs should be legalized. Even here, he has seen more heroin, where it is not supposed to be, than anywhere. There's booze here he said and drugs but he doesn't touch the stuff.

All this bores me.

We just sit next to each other, I lean into his chest, and we chat, four hours of chatting, some of it discussing our similarities, which on the surface are a lightheartedness, quickness, a desire to laugh, anywhere. But the undercurrent similarity is a powerful going to any end to run into oneself.

He is less flirtatious with me now that I am married. I don't know what we talk about the four hours but we do. Everyone knows a woman loves to be talked to. Any seducer knows that.

I have been here so often I now recognize the prisoners' babies.

"It's funny how I recognize the people here," I say. "They're always the same ones on the days I come."

David laughs, "That's not what it is, they visit often. They come more often than you do. You're like a ball player. I give you three strikes to get here."

"It was a home run today."

"Today," he says.

He is standing over me, smiling.

He never tries to French kiss me and I like him for that. He is not inappropriate in this inappropriate of places.

"I go back to my cell," he says, "and get mad about all the things I didn't say. What if we send each other a questionnaire," he says, "before our visits so we're prepared? For that easy off-the-cuff interview?"

I smile.

"What if there is ever a time," he says, "when we can just lie endlessly together and talk?"

He knows me. He knows I would like that.

"You don't drink a thing now?" he asks.

"Not a thing."

"That'll have to change. You've got to share wines with me."

I smile and nod in agreement, encouraging him, while knowing that I will never drink wine with him. I don't want to drink wine with anyone.

What I know is I am about to drive away from the prison, drive away from this flirtation, this high, this slight wine glow I get from being with him, I am driving away toward a sober, more grounded life.

CHAPTER 34

My husband and I are finally moving in together. He is like Samson, Hercules, Atlas, moving furniture up three flights of thin, dark stairs, rushing to put together futons, moving furniture and bookshelves he has made from room to room. He is tireless. I get exhausted watching. He bolts things in place. I don't trust his aesthetics, he tends to the cluttered. He tends to enclosure, put in as much as possible, then you will be safe. I am constantly standing there, "Don't block the light, don't block the light."

As each heavy box goes in, I think how can I leave, these would have to go out all over again. Then I tell myself when I leave him, it will be as if I am leaving for the proverbial coffee.

I will reinvent myself.

I may love the gentle trees and open courtyard from this apartment's kitchen and dining room, but there are other secrets, other apartments out there with their own gifts for me to explore. This is how I survive, around the next corner. In some ways, this gives me a young chin. I never settle down.

This morning he wants to have sex. He wakes with an erection, and his is the most beautiful of penises, there will never be one more beautiful, I admire it coldly and reverentially as I do sculpture, a work of art. I say, "I have to go to the ladies room first."

"Why?"

"I just do."

I don't want a baby. He is always pushing, trying to make the furniture heavier.

We have sex, me on my side and he almost lying down on top of me when we begin, and I push him off. I need air, I need to breathe, I need collection of my thoughts. I don't want some idiot huffing and puffing on top of me blocking my light. Does he think this is erotic pressing into me heavily as if I might lighten his burden?

Every man must stand alone my tautening arms say as I reposition us where we both can breathe.

I will miss living in my little home by myself. I will miss the

     To Any Lengths

mornings of pristine silence. They will always be there for me should I need them. I will miss the eroticization of my own life. Now I will have to engage.

My husband waves to me as he goes down the stairs to work. He is dressed in jeans and a torn t-shirt. He is going off to a carpentry shop to make an oak credenza for one of his clients and he will make us some end tables too. He is happy. He has a home.

I wave back and smile, I too am happy in spite of myself, even while sabotaging what I deem the demon of safety, even while keeping us on some edge that I think I must adhere to so we can find what layers lie there, even while believing I am mining truths that everyone does not want to know, even while being so-called sure that no one is trustworthy, worst of all and especially so myself, I am happy with suddenly having a home.

CHAPTER 35

My phone does not work and none of my office equipment is hooked up. I don't have a desk yet. My husband makes my desks for me, exquisite pieces that he recreates for each home, so now I sit over an ugly shaky cardboard table. In ways, this chaos is freeing. It's evil people who need order, they say. Make the outside surfaces impeccable. Like children's horror stories where the villain, in perfect tie with perfect pronunciation, disintegrates to a grotesque skull.

My husband and I disagree, as predicted, on the layout of the apartment. I am frightened to tell him a better approach so convinced I am he will sneer and not listen.

Last night before going to sleep in this enormous room which slopes down as if we are on a ship, we have never gone to sleep in this enormous a room, the traffic going loudly outside and a huge ugly bedroom piece with tinted glass across from us (part of the apartment), I said, "What if in the middle of the night that bedroom piece begins talking?"

"Wake me up," he said. "Are you scared?"

"Yes," I said. "I'm scared." As if I'm a kid. But I am kidding.

About love? Why is relationship so rarely the dizzying feeling of youth on a beach, when the sand and sea roses are yours, the seagulls squawking complicity and those first gropings were pure blue-sky perfection? One didn't need furniture and suitcases and all this clamoring together.

Here I am wondering if a strange piece of mammoth furniture may start talking.

In other words, I want something to happen.

He falls asleep.

I turn on my other side and realize I don't care if I lose all my business clients. Something new would happen.

I hear bells ringing, must be from St. Mark's Church whose clock does not match mine, but I believe St. Mark. I forget which one he was.

Old women slowly pass each other on the street below me carrying their black handbags, stopping at shop windows, putting their hands on their thick waists to peer in. Their stomachs move forward before them.

The sun is coming hot and unforgiving. It is September 1 and I got married July 17. I am now in a strange home.

David would say I am getting used to the bit. He is right. He talks about living in a huge place in New York when he gets out and in Pietrasanta as well. He will drive us in his Aston Martin to seven course dinners and to the villa he has rented for me. Obviously, he expects to be a millionaire when he gets out. "What do you think you'll do when you get out?" I ask.

"Oh, rob banks," he laughs, "although, I won't use you as a getaway car. You'd be twenty minutes late."

"No, really," I say.

"I don't know. I don't worry about money. I always make it."

I believe him. Anyone who wants to live well makes money.

"Do you have any money left?"

"Of course, I do."

The phone man is here. Friendly, helpful. I wonder how we would get along married. I am on the lookout everywhere for new husbands. Women must wonder about my husband that way when he goes to their apartments to do construction. Magicians of wiring and wood. The Ukranian landlords don't answer their door. Can I blame them?

The phone man works in the East Village and I tell him he must have some amazing stories working this area. "Especially near Alphabet City," he says. I want to ask him about those stories, but he has enough work to do.

He is busy working on the apartment. I always had a man help me when I moved. Even ex-lovers took the time to set me up. It was a given I was an incompetent.

Today, I read the life of Henry Miller to have a partner. Henry was a cool customer, a man who resisted progress for a very, very long time. A man who got in his own way. Till he finally got in his own way in the freest of terms.

Incompetents, like myself, have to learn how to use incompetence to advantage. It takes years to get over the sadness of being incompetent, long drawn out ungainly years, till finally, it becomes clear, one is incompetent in one thing to be competent in another.

CHAPTER 36

For the autodidact, transitions come hard. Henry spent years learning how to write, as do I. Oh, the noise here and yet Henry was learning while his wife prostituted for him. The selfishness we exact to realize ourselves. Or rather, the contortions to rev us. That voyeuristic prurience became his material. And where is mine hiding right in front of my nose?

An ex-lover visited me yesterday and told me his new girlfriend is very thoughtful, very attentive to him. "How?" I asked, thinking I would pick up some pointers from the young, his girlfriend. My ex-lover looked embarrassed and motioned to the telephone man crouched in the corner of the room working the wiring.

My ex-lover motioned, You can't be serious to discuss this now? Why not, I thought. It isn't as if the telephone man is a virgin. My mother would say.

I never found out his girlfriend's magic. But when the telephone man left, he asked me if I would be interested in having lunch some time.

Moving makes me miss my father. He gets further away with each move. Time elongates since his death. I am building a life he knows nothing of. After a while, as it did with him, the apartments will change more frequently, and it won't matter. I will have learned. I am no different than anyone else. One sails alone and consistently at the wheel.

I feel guilty I no longer seduce my husband as I did men in my youth. I remember the first man I lived with when I was young, very young. I remember moving with him to a large apartment. He eventually left that large apartment and I lived there alone, hearing noises and calling friends to quell my fear. But I remember when we moved in; I remember making love against the wall in the hallway. I was wearing thin plaid slacks and little t-shirts that I was always clad in in those days, my midriff showing. I remember this sort of sexual heat we were in for three or four years. I would pretend he had just picked me up hitch hiking or just met me in the apartment next door. We would play these games, something I never do with my husband. My first lover would take nude photos of me, he thought me beautiful, he said, and I believed it was I that was beautiful, not what I later learned, all young women.

Why do I have no interest in standing up against the hallway wall now?I would be thinking of bookshelves falling while he ripped away at my clothes, or did so and so call about the annual report, or when am I ever going to write well enough? That's what happens now. This morning as my husband woke, he rolled on top of me and I thought, Please please no not that I want to remember, stay in the cocoon, of my dream.

I suppose, in the old days, I was in the moment. Now I am only in my moment.

But when I moved into that large apartment with that first boyfriend, I knew I was passing through. That boyfriend was there to protect me, as even my husband is now. As was Henry Miller's wife. Protect me while I sort out what is my theme right in front of my nose.

CHAPTER 37

My husband waved to me this morning as he walked from the bathroom to the kitchen to make coffee. I was in bed as usual retrieving dreams.

He waved charmingly, as my father used to do.

I got up and weighed myself on the kitchen floor, since the bathroom slopes. My husband watched me summon the strength necessary to face a firing squad as I looked down to see what the scale's needle was up to. Yesterday it was high. Today it is low, and I am equally in disbelief.

"I don't know why you do it then," he says.

My husband watches this performance behind his lit camel.

Since the needle is low, I sit myself down naked and join him for a coffee. I remember how my father used to say he hated the way my mother went about naked. One time I helped my husband with a painting job and, because I had no painting clothes, I stood on the steel ladder, rolling the brushes, naked.

"I need a shepherd in this large apartment," I say. "We always had shepherds my father and I. Sputnik and Nikita Khrushchev."

"No," my husband says.

"Why not? It could eat all your old clothes. Delicious, he would say. My father had a passion for Russia. He wanted to call his youngest son Ivan but that wife wouldn't let him. Maybe he was a mole," and then I put my hands up to my face and scrunch up my nose, mole like.

My husband laughs.

My father and his lost creativity.

On that note, I take a bath and from the bath read to my husband Salinger's words which more or less went to the effect, that he was a paranoiac in reverse. He suspected the world of trying to make him happy.

It occurs to me I am allowing it myself.

I had sex last night and I won't be asked to star in any porno film, but I can say that I didn't push him away. I pretended he was David and that made it easier. Even though if it was ten years later with David, I would be pretending David was someone else.

As we went to sleep, my husband called me "buddy" and to my mind this bodes badly.

David sends a photo that he got from the prison chapel of French lovers kissing and says he would like to be doing that with me, in that place and time.

"Women who are nice to men in prison," my friend says, "are maternal."

Maternal? Maternal in the way the earth is maternal. In the way love as conceived as maternal is maternal. But it's not that. It's geography. Nowhere is prison if there is love. Everywhere is a prison if there isn't.

The noise on Second Avenue does not bother me this morning. The trees are waving in the sun, tropically. This afternoon we leave for the sea. David will receive my card with money in it and three nude women on the front.

We all get as much as we allow ourselves.

Nothing more.

CHAPTER 38

My shrink believes it is love that makes you creative. Haven't men with their revolving wives known that for years, love releases you from self-obsession.

"I am too self-obsessed to write successfully," I told the shrink.

"You keep holding on to get what you never got. That part of you is the survivor."

"Plenty of people with rough childhoods were creative. It's no excuse. Look at Charlie Chaplin."

"He probably didn't have as bad a childhood as you," the shrink said. "His mother was crazy, but she cared. Your mother is only crazy."

David calls and he sounds like he is founding a book-publishing firm in there. He is reading Piaget on child development, has written to a Foundation to get money for his child/prisoner communication book, enlisted the Bureau of Prisons and the head prison psychiatrist. They all want to be involved.

This guy is aggressive. He calls me at night when he knows my husband is home.

He says he will let me know what he needs.

"It's big, big," he said, "this thing. There's people in armed forces who want to communicate with their children; there's people in old age homes. This will solve our money problem. You won't need to worry anymore."

He knows how, as he says, to put a mission together.

"Oh, and send photos of yourself" he said. "I want to make you a drawing for your new apartment."

"Is it alright," he asks, "if I store my drawings with you? I can't keep them in my cell. The guards destroy them when they do checks."

"Sure, sure. Of course."

He wants to penetrate me.

Yet he never sends the drawings. It's an idea. Words to say on the phone.

I furtively pull aside the covers like a bad girl and get into bed with my husband after the phone call. Not that I was bad with my husband, which I am sure he would have liked. I want to be bad with the other guy. I suppose that is part and parcel of marriage anyway.

What will I do when David gets out? I imagine myself telling my group therapy, I've never mentioned this but there's a man in prison and there's something amazing between us and do I have permission to leave now? Some of the men would ask what his prospects are exactly. The women would squirm in their seats and think what a childhood she must have had to fear getting close this much. Why didn't they have one like it?

Last night my shrink asked me why I don't marry someone like himself. I said, "What would someone like myself hatched in a dark bar say to your tennis partners?"

"Are you invested in making our marriage work?" my husband says to me in the bath this morning.

"Are you?"

"Don't answer a question with a question."

"Yes," I say guiltily.

I told David that I will be out on parole in January. Six months. The phone at FCI got disconnected just then so we didn't have time to argue a date.

"You're my easiest patient," my shrink says. "You're content with crumbs. You never ask for anything."

I lie there embarrassed. Well, what am I supposed to ask for?

"I want," I say haltingly, "encouragement. You know, to come out from the corner."

"Express your feelings for me then."

"That again."

I don't say it, but I have a vision then on the couch. Of me expressing my feelings by running in front of a train to prove my point. See? I'll show you. Here comes the train.

Maybe he's right; there hasn't been enough love in my life.

CHAPTER 39

Thanksgiving came and went with my husband's family. They provided a wood stove not crackling off enormous heat but enough to assuage one from complaining. They provided non-intrusive classical music (I never understand why people do that, either you want to hear music as a living breathing entity, or you don't,) creamed onions, the right amount precisely of carved turkey, apple pie with vanilla ice cream, conversation dotted-with-hopeful laughter.

We brought too sweet non-alcoholic wine.

I have spent Thanksgiving with them for the past ten years. Before that, I never went anywhere.

After the meal that seemed to take days, I notice it is still afternoon. I tell my husband I want to go to our motel room over the Camden Harbor and write.

"Are you crazy?" he responds.

All of a sudden, I will suffocate if I cannot be without the guards of proprietary around me. I must go out on the page.

"Can't you take one day off?"

"No."

He lights a camel. He sneers. "You love writing more than you love me."

"It's not a competition. I . . . I just want to spend a few hours in the hotel room. You can talk with your cousins. Your aunt. You don't need me here."

"You always have to go off," he spits out, standing tall above me. "You can never just be part of, acquiesce, go with. No, no you have to go off, be independent."

Well, yes.

"It's just a few hours," I say.

"So give them up."

"If I do," I say, "I will be off key. My system needs it. It's how I process."

"Process with us. Me. Learn to be intimate."

At this point, the turkey, the fire, the dining room are moth wings covering me. I think of the night I spent once sleeping in the Camden cemetery, when I went to meet him at his aunt's and he didn't hear me knocking. He and his aunt had locked the front door. No one answered the phone. I slept alone in the cemetery, tending my rage and loneliness ecstatically.

I wave my hands in the air. "Just let me go," I say.

He throws the car keys at me. "Here," he says to the floor.

"I'll be back before you know it," I say and try to kiss his neck. He jerks away.

I say, "See you soon" when I go into the living room to his aunt and his cousins who don't seem bothered in the least by my disappearance for two hours. His aunt will take a nap and the cousins may even talk to each other.

Charlie manages somehow to not look at me while glowering at me. If I didn't feel so sad, I would study how he does that.

I am glad he wants me to stay, might even say I need it, but I can't.

That night I dream the prisoner and I are defiantly walking through the prison hallway, past the other cells. He is wearing a Daniel Boone raccoon hat with a striped tail down the back.

CHAPTER 40

David calls and I can't get my voice into that slight delight-edness that he calls sexy till I am sure my husband is sure I'm talking to someone else.

David says his book is going well, all of a sudden everyone I know is writing books, what it is we spawn around us, and for some reason it hurts me since everyone has the drive and talent I do not have, everyone else has enough anger to spurt out their work.

David says, "Well how seriously do you want to be involved in this book I'm doing?"

"What will it entail?" I ask.

"Oh at least twenty or thirty years of your life," he says.

"Okay," I say huskily, "you got it."

"Lots of person to person meetings with me," he says. "By the way," he asks, "how does your sentence work, do you get resentenced after 6 months? Another indictment?"

He tells me he just got out of the hole. Something about a warden change and too much stuff in his cell. Five days. He thinks everyone should do solitary at some point.

I listen to his version of solitary and my mind wanders to those people forced to emigrate and not able to understand a word of English.

Women in therapy tired of being alone.

David tells me his wife thinks the book idea is excellent, and she never likes any scheme he has.

"Are you going to marry her again when you get out?" I ask.

"Baby I'm never getting married again."

"You mean you won't marry me?"

He laughs. Caught.

"Baby, I'll live with you when I get out."

That shrink he ruins everything. Now living together won't be enough.

"The thing is," I tell the shrink, "I don't have a heart. I didn't grow one. There's a hole there. Why would my husband marry someone without a heart?"

"He must not have a brain," he says.

"Hah. Well he's going to want someone with a heart eventually."

"I want to make love," I say to the shrink, "I don't want it to be impossible to surrender. And what's even worse is that by the time you transfer a bit of your heart to me and I am able to make love, I'll be too old no one will want me. I will be too old to begin a career."

"Shaw," he says, "was 50 when he wrote his first book."

(They all tout Shaw at these times.)

"Gauguin," the shrink continues, "went off to Tahiti at 45."

Everybody knows that. But think. The pictures came out when he had tossed all distraction, the all-repressing of himself, when he let fly his true sight. That's when he got the work. Not before. Before he had talent. Everyone has talent. Once he let himself be truly himself, he had work.

Yes, yes I will persevere, I say to the shrink and to anyone else who asks. No one does ask. They are too busy asking themselves.

"Do you mean," I ask, "that my inability to get close to a man is my inability to embrace my own creativity? My elusiveness is not from them, but from myself."

He nods, even though my back is turned to him on the couch.

"Do you mean that the real relationship for me is to my own fire and the rest is distraction?"

He nods, even though my back is turned to him on the couch.

"Do you mean that all of this is nonsense? Yes, we need love and so on but the primary engagement is with one's own eros?"

Here he hesitates. He wants to disagree. Love and work and all of that. He wants to tell me to acclimate, but he knows he spends fourteen hours a day in his analyst chair. Then he goes home. Only then.

He nods, even though my back is turned to him on the couch.

"Do you mean that I have to go for my own wildness, my own being? I cannot be what Charlie or David want. I can only be this."

Silence.

"Do you mean that I am alone and that is who I am? Alone, answering to my own Gods and happy."

He nods, even though my back is to him on the couch.

CHAPTER 41

"What was your day like?" my husband asks from the bath where he is trying to rub soot off himself from having worked on someone's fireplace. He dips his head completely under the water and snorts into it, then resurfaces still snorting. He must be most uncomfortable in the bath, kneeling over like that, as if waiting for his dead mother to wash his back.

"You don't want to know, it was too nice," I say.

"No tell me, it makes this all worthwhile."

"I wrote. I exercised. I did a bit of commercial work. I'm trying to write more pages each day since Tom says I need lots of pages. But it doesn't amount to more, I just end up cutting more."

I don't mention that I also went to an afternoon movie. That would be almost lewd given how hard he is working.

"Wow," he says, "you wrote 10 pages. Amazing."

"Well, they're not that good. I'm reading Wideman and he makes me want to pack the whole thing in. Why didn't I think to tell David's story, counterpoint? Wideman goes into the subject. Next time I'll show characters. Next time I'll tell the truth."

He is running more water, splashing his bath all over the bathroom floor. He does not hear me.

He is working very hard, I have to admit, paying off what seems to be an endless stream of debts. Marriage, car, a house, taxes—all responsibilities I consider solely his. I travel light. I'll pay my own taxes, but I don't take on all those possessions. I watch him, appalled at his being willing to weigh himself down like that.

"Maybe I should get a job," I say.

"Don't compete with me."

"Jesus. I'm not competing with you. I'm trying to help out."

"No you write and wait and see what happens. I'll come out of this."

Instead of responding, I do a quick searchlight glare round the kitchen for cockroaches. My war against the species God gave eternal life to.

Do I believe him? I ask the cockroaches.

They answer back, What other choice do you have?

"Give it some time," says the humpback in the bath.

Endure, say the cockroaches.

David wants me to visit him and for some reason I cannot bring myself to go. This is new. I am not garnering sexual tension from him anymore. I am angry at him for being there. He is doing more solitary, he says, he will tell me why when I see him. He's a revolutionary he says. "Come here," he says, "I will solve all your problems. I've got the answers."

"To everything?" I ask.

"Just get your ass here. You're the only visit I enjoy. The minister who came asked me if I am going bald. He told me I won't be able to move back to my hometown. They must learn these ways of communicating in the ministry. You've gotta come here, we can't have a relationship if we don't see each other."

Why is it my responsibility?

"I asked them when they will move me to low security, they said not for a while." He laughs.

"What are you doing in there to get into solitary so much? Are women trying to break in to see you? Is that it?"

He laughs and oh it does my heart good to hear someone

locked up laugh.

This morning I woke earlier than my husband and stared at what seemed an African sunrise from the bedroom window. It was so profuse, so orange on this winter day. I looked at that burning sky and realized my husband is getting healthier. I have a person here to deal with. He wants me to respond to him sexually, he wants me, in other words, to love him.

"Well, it's research," a friend says about visiting David.

"Oh, the hell with that research," I say.

There's another research, the research of living within my own life.

David says I am happier away from my husband and I am sure this is true. But that does not simply mean to leave my husband. I am always unhappy in the pinch of other people. How to hold my chest out.

I didn't roll over and make love with my husband as the sun came up. I snuggled in, rubbed my leg against his. I didn't make the effort. He held me. Earlier that day he had called me because he was a bit depressed at work. I said, "Do you have field mice in your head?"

"That's it," he said.

I was amazed he was liking himself enough to want me to

love him. This is what marriage has done. It has given us a home, the one his dead parents and my deadened parents couldn't give. So now with a little protection, we're coming awake.

What am I to do with such progress?

CHAPTER 42

My husband bolted in a new sturdy desk for me last night. He was struggling and pushing wires through the desk holes he had bored, reaching over the edge, even with his bad back. Big and strong this desk is, able to withstand my space ship lamp, the one plant a rubber plant he gave me which keeps growing dispelling my myth that nature and I are incompatible, the calculator that tells a web of sorrow to my checkbook, the fax that is now indispensable. He made the big red and wooden desk and installed it himself. Carried it up the three flights of stairs, even with his bad back.

My friend says, "Now go make him dinner."

I go out and get food from the Polish restaurant nearby. Lamb shank and noodles. I heat it in the foil container.

I can see the clock on St Mark's if I lean back. He even thought to put the chair that way. The heater at my back. It is warm outside and that too is a gift. People saunter by in their shabby jackets carrying newspapers. Foreign men get out of second-hand rusted cars to buy cigarettes. Their thin elegance makes me think they're on their way to hotel desk jobs. Fat women walk their dogs or march forward with their Walkman ears on. A dazed foreigner goes by carrying his stuffed suitcase.

I am leaving this morning to retrieve his car, which is being fixed at a gas station 200 miles away. On the way home, I notice his radio does not work. I stop at a Radio Shack and buy a cheap boom box. Now I am driving back to New York swiftly and freely, singing at the top of my voice. Tomorrow is my birthday and I think of all the things I want to do in my life: live in Paris, go through the mountains of Austria, talk to other people than my husband. I think of how much I need to believe in myself. How I need to not agree so quickly with rejections I receive. I drive along and tell myself I should defend my work, not abandon it. I pull out a pen and paper from my purse and make a note to reread what I have written and see if there are stories there. I am not going to lie down and give up so easily. I will stand up.

I am driving along the highway, changing the station whenever there is an announcer, continually looking out the rear view mirror for the police, when all of a sudden, as they say, I see smoke. An enormous amount of smoke hiding the hood.

My husband, whose mother died in a car crash when he was a child, has owned 24 cars and all of them blow up in one-way or another. Car repair shops are ineffectual against my husband's karma.

Immediately and fortunately I pull off the highway down the ramp and roll in behind smoke to a roadside gas station. The young kid on duty tells me he just pumps gas; he knows nothing about cars and is about to close up.

"Can I use the phone?"

He nods disinterestedly.

My husband does not answer.

The young kid comes back and lets me know tomorrow morning someone can look at it. As the young kid barely finishes giving his lackluster information, a young man in a souped-up white Cadillac comes over to me like Clint Eastwood. I tell him my story. This young man seems interested. He officiously walks to my husband's car and lifts the hood to look at the engine. He twists over one way. He twists over another way. He talks to

     To Any Lengths

himself. Then he closes the hood and turns to me, "The engine seized. You better stay in a motel down the street. I'll drive you."

The night before my birthday and indeed I can't think of anything I'd like more than to be alone in a motel room down the street.

From my room, I call my husband. He apologizes. I say, "It's not your fault."

I do not have enough money for more than a diet coke, what with buying the boom box that afternoon. Tomorrow I will find a bank and take the train to New York. Tomorrow is my birthday.

"We'll do something together," he says.

That feels wonderful too.

I am alone, free, in a hotel room, with my life before me. The vicissitudes of marriage have broken down and I am to spend the night quietly and widely in my imagination. I am, as Henry said, the happiest woman alive.

CHAPTER 43

Peter Handke's words THERE IS ONLY ROOM FOR
THOSE WHO MAKE ROOM FOR THEMSELVES.

My husband and I have that birthday dinner in a Japanese
restaurant next door that is offering a discount on sushi. Speaking
of birthdays, he has something to bring up.

He wants a child.

I don't tell him I am a child and the child I want is the child
within me to become simple and hear.

He tells me that now we are married I must settle down and
tell him exactly how much money I owe. I must consider living

where we can afford it. He wants to look at a little house outside of New York on a middle-class street.

"This is what people do," he says.

"We just moved here," I say.

"New York is too expensive."

"I know. But the aliveness, the imagination—"

"It's too expensive."

I nod. It is.

I suddenly see. I see it all before me. He wants to return to the sea town where he came from because it is affordable and he likes sailing more than he likes overpriced restaurants. But I won't be able to leave this solitary life of mine. He's going alone.

It is written, was always written. He will meet someone else with whom he will have a child. We are at the beginning of the ending, as my mother predicted. We are at the beginning of his making room for himself.

I say, "What about moving to Gloucester, to your house?"

"You hate it," he responds.

"Not more than some middle-class street that is nowhere. At least Gloucester has beauty."

He brightens like it is his birthday.

The snake in me says, "You could go there. I mean, we."

"Try and pronounce we."

I smile sadly.

"We should go to my house," he says. "The mortgage is nothing."

I nod.

"We have to accumulate things," he says. "Material. A family. A house. You don't do that but that is what people do."

What happened to the Marxist poet's son? Did I have us confused?

"Maybe you could live in your house, if you prefer it," I say, "and I could live here and we could commute. The best of both worlds. The best of a marriage."

To my surprise, he nods.

I thought it would take longer.

We both knew it was going to happen. He married me to complete this and now he is on to the next thing. I am losing him and this slight chance I had at a home.

Portrait of an artist as a consummate fool.

CHAPTER 44

My husband is reading the paper. He said he was going to work but he is not.

I can hear the pages of his newspaper turn from my office.

Last night he called me "a mad queen." This because I wore a long black dress when we walked to watch the dogs play in the dog run. He points out to me that the sign says No owners without dogs. I walk in anyway. I come into my own where chaos flourishes.

I tried to write a letter this morning, what I do to start my day, but my concentration was on the sound of his refusing to leave the house. I am under house arrest.

The phone rings with a woman wanting to talk about problems. I cannot talk with my husband listening and, in truth; I don't want to talk about problems. I want to alchemize them at my desk.

My husband did not go to work yesterday either. He said they don't need him.

I said, "Let's go on the Circle Line at lunchtime." I want to show him Hell's Gate from the water. But instead he chose the one-hour Circle Line—the one that runs the same route as the Staten Island Ferry.

Even an hour on a field trip is good, so off we went. But there is no imagination on this tourist trip. The Statue of Liberty is prosaic. I remark, "It's interesting how the statue is so powerful because there is not much symbolism. It is direct, like a Greek statue," which was prosaic of me. The prosaic brings about the prosaic and this is what I have been warning everyone about in these pages.

I would rather have been sailing at my desk. I did it to entertain him as one would a child. I did it to get him out of the house. I went with him to be polite. I was polite because I feel such rage.

     To Any Lengths

I buy him a hot dog on the boat. And then pay for a cab for us to come straight home. He says, "You have expensive tastes." He goes out for a walk when we get home, but it is not enough.

I cannot work anyway.

I go looking at clothes I cannot afford. I buy one dress that I lie to him about the price of. I cut it down by $200.

In bed I worry that I am too old for such a dress. A sundress like I am a young girl. I had forgotten my age in my exuberance at being alone.

I take a drive after going shopping. This in Manhattan. No one goes for drives in Manhattan. I take a drive to see the sun on the river. I race the car down Harlem River Drive. My husband might even be standing there by the water, looking at the strong, difficult currents.

Currents that require a tugboat for order.

Even though we love each other, I think we are planning something.

When he returns, I say, "What's the matter?"

"You're preoccupied," he says.

"How do you mean?"

"You can't sit still."

That seems to be true.

"Something must be bothering me," I reply.

"What?"

"I don't know. That I am broke," I say, "I can't find work and neither can you, that I don't want to work and neither do you, that we both would rather be playing and I don't understand why we can't be playing, I don't, and I don't understand why we both feel so alone even though we are together and I don't understand how this aloneness is such a terrible weight and I can't get rid of it nor do I want to. I don't understand why I am a failure at real life."

He looks aghast at me. Then he screams at me, "I didn't want that big an answer. Just be patient and let me help us. I'll make money and everything will be alright."

"But it can't just be money—" I say. I, who worry about money all the time.

"It is," he says. And I know he says that because he doesn't want to deal with whatever else it might be.

"You never see," he says, "the power of the practical."

That night I sleep on the couch because I want to dream alone. My dreams are better when I sleep alone. I sleep alone longing for the peace of mind to sleep with him.

CHAPTER 45

My husband is putting the sails up. This is his first boat, a wooden boat that sat out on an old codger's lawn for years. For six months, my husband visited him whenever he was by the sea to ask this man if he'd sell his boat. Finally, the owner got sick of my husband's asking. So here I am watching my husband struggle, as he likes to, to get the mainsail up.

I watch his tall handsomeness, the focus with which he battles the elements. I have seen him thus wrestle with bicycles, ice skates, our conversations.

The sun is not fully out. He says, "It'll just be a few seconds" and he keeps pulling at the main sail.

I look around the harbor, at this fishing town on a hill. It is beautiful, my husband's home.

Finally, he gets the sail up and we motor out to sea. My husband is happy at the helm, waving to people he knows on other boats. I sit at the other end of the boat, where he has told me to, and he smiles at the sea, at the mast, at the till, at me.

I enjoy it. I enjoy watching him enjoy it. But as the clouds thicken, I can't help noticing, and wishing I didn't, that I miss, just a bit, the streets back home where we live.

CHAPTER 46

My husband walks into the apartment.

"I'm in my office," I yell from the bathtub.

I am sweaty from the hot water and am laying my book down on the wet tiles, as he stands at the bathroom door. My hair is up but strands fall down wet around my neck.

"How was your day at the office?" I ask.

"People are idiots," he says. "No one should have to work for a living."

I look at him and say nothing.

"Need any money?" he asks.

"Nope" I say.

"When are you going to take something from me?"

"Your youth wasn't enough?"

"Hey," my husband says, "I don't complain."

He goes and sits down at the kitchen table. Runs his hands through his hair.

I come to him in a towel and put my arms around him.

"I love you," I say. He knows I love him, but he stays hard and immobile to my touch. I must not think I can get away with everything.

"You're a freedom fighter. You don't do as I say," he explains when I ask why he is angry.

I look confused at him.

He is not joking.

He has taken to going to his other house more often, the one in the country. I am going there less and less, except when it is summer, and I want to be outside. The house doesn't have a garden and that is something I can't keep from noticing. It is true that part of my husband's attractiveness had been that he owned a house. He was tangible. He would outlast time. I would have a home with him. A home to come home to.

I had loved, it's true, that my husband was building a house, not a bar tab.

However, I never liked spending time in the house. The house was too settled, too staid, too terrifying in its need for kitchen grains, dishes, and woman's work.

"Let's get on our bikes," I'd say, "and go to the beach."

"Let me finish the floor."

Now I am more often in the city by myself. He is more often in the house he has built.

As with the prisoner, my husband is being relegated to the phone.

"I hate to tell you this," he says on our nightly call from his house, "but I'm retiling the upstairs bathroom. I'm going to throw out the bathtub."

"That's alright."

"Well I'm going to bed now," he says.

"That's it?" I ask somewhat joking.

"That's it."

"Talk to you tomorrow."

Throwing out the bathtub. I'll probably be next.

"Why do you still visit him?" my husband asks, when we are once again together in New York.

"I find it interesting."

"Why?"

"Being locked up. How you find freedom in it."

"I don't like it," my husband says.

"It's harmless."

"The guy's conning you."

"Into what? He's going to be in forever."

"He just likes to con. He can't help it."

"All men do," I say.

"You're wrong," my husband says. "Do you think I con you?"

"No. But you conned yourself into thinking you want a wife. You really want a mother. To watch you sail."

He laughs. "All men want a mother."

"Some men want a friend."

"Don't be ridiculous. I want that too," he says. "But all men want a mother."

My husband loses interest at this point and opens his book on sailing up the Amazon. He interrupts me to ask me how to pronounce a word in Japanese. I don't speak Japanese. When I say, I don't know, his face gets annoyed as if I am hiding it from him.

For some reason, I even feel a twinge of guilt over not telling him what I do not know.

CHAPTER 47

When my husband arrives back in the city from his house, he has a Playboy in his suitcase. "Don't get upset," he says, "I've been using them for years."

I look down at his open bag and say nothing.

I know these pictures disappoint him less than I do.

I smile, kiss him, and walk back to my office. He uses Playboy. I use my writing.

CHAPTER 48

The next night he tells me not to worry about the mistakes I make at work. He will take care of me. I am not alone in the world.

I follow him to the kitchen and run my hands through his hair while he talks on his phone and he shoves me away. I kiss his neck and he jerks his head to push me off.

My husband. He has his grievances.

He comes back into the living room where I sit cross-legged, smoking a cigarette, waiting for him.

"When are you going to have a baby?" he asks.

I look at him and want to say, I already have one. Me.

"If you're not going to give me a baby," he continues, "you should at least be willing to live in the country with me."

I nod.

"We're not getting anywhere," he says. He is still standing, looking down at me.

"Where are we trying to go?" I ask.

"We should be moving forward."

I nod but I don't want to go wherever it is married people go. Haven't I made that clear to everyone?

"I am not good at marriage," I say. "I have stuff I feel I have to do here."

He leaves the room in disgust.

I follow him to the bedroom where his back is turned toward me. As I walk through the apartment, I pass framed photographs of him that I have taken. He looks angry. Then I realize he looks angry because he is looking at the woman taking the picture. That woman is me.

CHAPTER 49

My phone rings constantly. One woman whose foot is healing distracts herself from her pain by meeting men over match.com. She says they are redneck types. She lives in Vermont. One of these men, she says, owns five houses, is a CEO and she will contact him to see how she fares with a successful man.

I feel nothing.

Another friend offers to take me to a play while her husband plays bridge. She rarely spends time with her husband and likes to spend time with me.

I feel nothing.

A woman writer who was a therapist wants to have lunch.

She is sixty years old and consumed in how her mother hurt her. A man wants to talk about his comedy act and I don't. The hairdresser says he will come tomorrow.

There is no time for commerce.

An agent friend calls. How is David? How is my husband? She is on her cell phone, buying oranges, en route to her broker. She has money with many brokers so no one knows how much money she has. If she picked men like she picked oranges, she would be fine, she says.

When my husband was here, I marshaled my time more carefully. Time for him. Time for me. Now I just give it away to the ten thousand myriad forms so as not to be alone.

The bookstore calls to tell me Without Child is here. An old friend who has just moved to San Francisco tells me I forgot his birthday. He is dating hundreds of women. He says they all have something that is attractive. I say that is the way with a harem. I dislike him because he never feels anything.

A woman is sad because the school system where she teaches sabotages her. I try to imagine her as a teacher, a woman whose speech I can hardly understand. She is always railing against the system, pushing, pushing for more, for more. Later David will call. And even if my husband does not call, his not calling will buzz louder in my mind than if he does.

What I am telling you is that rejection keeps you busier than anything.

To Any Lengths

CHAPTER 50

Seneca says Keep a guilt-free conscience. You suffer the pangs of detection even when undetected. He says only go after the fruits of philosophy. Money and all the rest are transient and easily lost and, worse, rob you of your time in their demands.

Be able, he says, to live with nothing else but wisdom.

It is men who have asked me to own and be owned. I have continually said No, let me think.

Yet Seneca talks of loving himself vicariously through his wife's love.

I am happy visiting my husband this weekend. I can hear the rain, but the curtains are closed. The fire is crackling, and I can see trees from the windows without curtains. For how long I would like this monastery, I do not know. For the moment, it is, like every moment, pure pleasure.

I will finish reading Seneca, who apparently could not live by his own philosophies. He could only write them. His own life was derailed, apparently, by desire. He spent his life writing of the fight against desire. He has not admitted yet that he has lost. He says instead to be stalwart toward our own death.

I write constantly of the desire for union. While I hover outside the door. This is true philosophy. This studying of, not perhaps living, freedom. Freedom comes in the most surprising of ways. Only death does what it is supposed to do.

CHAPTER 51

When I am back in the city, a young woman on the phone asks me, "What are you going to do?"

She means about my marriage.

I stammer out an attempt at response. The truth is I don't know.

I had a pleasant weekend with my husband. He worked on the car, he fed me. He bought me a pair of earrings I picked out. He paid for the gifts I had to buy. We had dinners and lunches with friends of ours. He carried the picnic blankets. He took my friend's husband out for a test drive in his car. We simulated being a couple.

We made love at the end of the weekend.

He looked at my naked body and said, "I can tell if you have been cheating."

But he couldn't.

He looked at me when we made love. He cupped my face and I hung my head back over the side of the bed. I squeezed my eyes shut.

I fell peaceably asleep in his arms after.

I called another man on the way home and said, "I miss you."

I don't know what I am going to do.

CHAPTER 52

The man who opens the cleaners is crossing the street. He is working, as I must. Seems I am living the life of the divorcee. I must compete with people who are building careers, not, like myself, hoping to end them.

A girl with beautiful legs speed walks by. A girl sat yesterday in the sun, her legs poured out on the concrete steps, and the men's eyes like runaway trains.

A year ago, I would have driven this Memorial Day weekend to see my husband. But he says he is working and I say I am doing the same.

Last night I tell a poet friend a story. About stories. I say I loved my husband for his being the son of a poet, the 8-year-old orphan of a mother killed in a car crash. I fell in love with that story, the Molotov cocktail of loneliness, abandonment, the sea, and the memory of my father in that sea town. I tell the poet I fell in love with the prisoner, doing time in solitary, the Vietnam war hero, the gun chrome blue eyes, the hard body of handsome words. I fell in love with the story.

But my husband and the prisoner, they kept saying, "Be with me.Right here."

I could not leave their stories.

I did not want to be a woman serving coffee and my time to them. I wanted to stay in the swell of the stories.

My husband and the prisoner got lonely. "Commit," they yelled. "I need a woman in the car beside me. In bed next to me. Not in her imagination."

"I can't," I said, terrified.

"How do you feel now?" The poet asked.

"Happy," I answered. "I think I do want to come into prosaic, boorish reality. But I don't know how to. I do know the stories leave not only the men lonely, but me too."

"Well whom will you do it with?" The poet said, his eye

     To Any Lengths

gleaming. In his own story.

"I don't know. Might start my own."

CHAPTER 53

This morning there was an accident on the Tappan Zee Bridge. The traffic stopped. I read Nâzim Hikmet at my steering wheel.

When we got going, it wasn't long before I got stopped again. By the police for speeding. It was the music on the radio, a sexual beat that had me racing.

"You can contest these tickets," the engineers tell me when I finally get to work. But what would I say?

God knows I would like to stand in that New York upstate courtroom and talk of the heart soaring unexpectedly. How there is no cure for it. I would like to argue with the officer who would respond, "What if everybody's heart soared unexpectedly on the road?"

What would happen?

People would stop for more ice creams.

People would slow down to enjoy the fir trees and valleys. People would somberly bury the deer at the side of the road. People would make love in the back seat.

What if we all drove to the speedometer of our hearts?

Mayhem would be in the rejoicing.

CHAPTER 54

Ah, how Hikmet, the writer-prisoner, offered encouragement to his countrymen, to his fellow prisoners, to his wife. How at fifty he says he became a mailman in Hungary after wanting to be a mailman as a child. As a child, he fantasized delivering the encouraging letter in the nick of time to a suffering family. In prison, he wrote poems, hundreds of poems.

"And who knows,

The woman you love may stop loving you.

Don't say it's no big thing:

It's like the snapping of a green branch

    To the man inside.

To think of roses and gardens inside is bad,

To think of seas and mountains is good.

Read and write without rest,

And I also advise weaving

And making mirrors.

I mean, it's not that you can't pass

Ten or fifteen years inside

                       And more—

You can,

As long as the jewel

On the left side of your chest doesn't lose it's luster!"

Yes, I failed. But I lived, as Hikmet's wife. As David's totem. As the streets' ambassadress. Generous as only the amoral can be. It wasn't, it never was my husband or David I could not commit to, it was always, always to dreaming. "Take out the dress I first saw you in,

Look your best,

Look like spring trees...

Wear in your hair

The carnation I sent you in a letter from prison,

Raise your kissable, lined, broad white forehead.

Today, not broken and sad—

No way!—

Today Nâzim Hikmet's woman must be beautiful

Like a rebel flag..."

   To Any Lengths

CHAPTER 55

"Did you flirt with anyone at work today?" the prisoner asks me on the phone.

"I never flirt," I say flirtatiously.

"Oh right," he laughs.

"Well how does one flirt?" I ask. "Give me some tips. I forget."

"You flash your eyes and you smile a big smile. Just do what you normally do," he says.

"You've known me over nine years," I say to the prisoner, "and name one time you've seen me flirt. Name one time."

He thinks and says he can't remember. I am surprised since in my mind I am flashing my eyes all the time, even at garbage cans. He can't come up with anything, because he is trying to shut out that it is all I do with him.

It is all I do lately with everything.

CHAPTER 56

Last night my husband says to me on the cell phone as I am driving up there, "The suburbs are boring. I've got to get out of here." What I heard was, "That terrifies you doesn't it?"

When I arrive at his house we talk about this one's personality, that one's, and how my hair has a long way to go but when we get into bed and are finally quiet, he says, "You can't be married. You could never be happy with one man. Nobody could take it."

"Are you saying you can't take it?"

"Oh I can," he lies. "It's just I wish we were together more."

When Sunday comes, I get in the car to return home. He is at his.

We are drifting apart.

We tried, to merge. But like many tales of love and loss, we turned out to be a story. When we could not infuse it with any more imagination, the story ended. When the prisoner was no longer weaving and preening in my mind, that story ended. When it was my imagination that claimed me, became mine and mine to follow, the story began.

ABOUT THE AUTHOR

British born, Montreal raised, New York City honed, JACQUELINE GAY WALLEY, under the pen name Gay Walley, has been publishing short stories since 1988 and published her first novel, *Strings Attached*, with University Press of Mississippi (1999), which was a Finalist for the Pirates Alley/ Faulkner Award and earned a Writer's Voice Capricorn Award and the Paris Book Festival Award. *The Erotic Fire of the Unattainable: Aphorisms on Love, Art and the Vicissitudes of Life* was published by IML Publications in 2007 and was reissued by Skyhorse Publishing 2015. This book, *The Erotic Fire of the Unattainable* was a finalist for the Paris Book Festival Award and from this, she wrote a screenplay for the film, *The Unattainable Story* (2016) with actor, Harry Hamlin, which premiered at the Mostra Film Festival in Sao Paolo, Brazil. Walley also wrote a screenplay for director Frank Vitale's docufiction feature film, *Erotic Fire of the Unattainable: Longing to be Found* (2020), which was featured in Brooklyn Film Festival, Sarasota Film Festival, Cinequest Film & Creativity Festival in San Jose, ReadingFilmFest, and American Fringe in Paris (2020). Her novel, *Lost in Montreal* (2013) was published by Incanto Press, along with the novel, *Duet*, which was written with Kurt Haber. Walley's e-books, *How to Write Your First Novel, Save Your One Person Business from Extinction*, and *The Smart Guide to Business Writing* are featured on Bookboon, as well as *How to Keep Calm and Carry on Without Money* and

How to be Beautiful available on Amazon. In 2013, her play *Love, Genius and a Walk* opened in the Midtown Festival, New York, and was nominated for 6 awards including best playwright, in 2018, it also played in London at The Etcetera Theatre above The Oxford Arms pub as well as at three other pub theatres. It is scheduled to open in 2021 in Theatro Techni in London. In October 2021, Jacqueline Gay Walley's 6 novel *Venus as She Ages* Collection – *Strings Attached* (second edition, under her pen name, Gay Walley), *To Any Lengths, Prison Sex, The Bed You Lie In, Write She Said*, and *Magnetism* – is being launched worldwide through IML Publications and distributed by Ingram.

Since IML's humble erratic beginnings, the mascot, which has reverently danced across our newsletter, the watermarks of the website, the original interiors, and now these front and back pages, is a graphic symbol of the Kalahari San Bushmen's Trickster God, the praying mantis, who has forever—or for as long as they can remember—been inspiring the mythological stories of these First People who nomadically walk the earth whenever they can, as our nomad authors write their way through life.